A FRIEND IN NEED, MARY BROWN

A NOVELLA

BERNICE BLOOM

DEAR READERS

So, where were we then? Oh yes...lovely Mary and Ted are embarking on a new life together. They are moving into their new flat on a gorgeous little street in Hampton Court.

Life is pretty wonderful until they get a call from Mary's best friend, Charlie.

Charlie needs help. She's found a box marked 'confessions', and it contains lots of things that threaten to ruin her relationship. Mary will have to go to all sorts of extraordinary lengths to help her. And what's Ted's role in all this? Is he part of the mystery that Mary's desperate to solve?

I hope you enjoy it

Lots of love, BB xx

THE MARY BROWN BOOKS IN ORDER

1. WHAT'S UP, MARY BROWN?
2. THE ADVENTURES OF MARY BROWN
3. CHRISTMAS WITH MARY BROWN
4. MARY BROWN IS LEAVING TOWN
5. MARY BROWN IN LOCKDOWN
6. MYSTERIOUS INVITATION
7. A FRIEND IN NEED
8. DOG DAYS FOR MARY BROWN
9. DON'T MENTION THE HEN WEEKEND
10. THE ST LUCIA MYSTERY

SPECIAL NOTE:

This book was previously released as 'Confessions of an Adorable Fat Girl' but now has a new name and a sparkling new cover.

A FRIEND IN NEED, MARY BROWN

1

Isn't the summer an absolute joy? A time of glorious colours etched across the landscape with a richness and vibrancy that makes you want to leap up, throw off your clothes, and run like a wild thing through the fields before leaping into a cool waterfall.

Not that I'd ever do that, of course. I have a body that resembles uncooked dough. I'd rather run across hot coals than run anywhere naked. I'm just saying that it's a gorgeous time, full of exciting possibilities and hope for brighter, happier, more fulfilling days ahead.

'This weather is wonderful,' I shout over to Juan as I lift my face into the sunshine and smile over at the roses coming into late summer bloom.

'Really? Do you like this? I'm sweating like a snowman in a sauna.'

'I thought you adored summer?'

'Yes, it's a joy when I'm by a pool in Spain, with an air-conditioned apartment nearby and no work to do. Not like today when I have lots of heavy lifting to do. Do you need all this damn stuff?'

He is staggering down the rough stone steps outside my house as we speak, holding a pile of faded Russian dolls, a giant sombrero and an oboe.

'Yes, I need it all,' I say, ushering him to place it gently in the van.

'I've never seen you play with these Russian dolls. Nor have I seen you playing the oboe while wearing a sombrero. Why would you even have an oboe? Who plays the oboe? Such a silly instrument.'

'They had run out of flutes at school.' I explain. 'Cathy Jenkins took the last flute, even though it was promised to me. I had to play the oboe. It's a sore point; let it go.'

He places the sombrero on my head and flicks it dismissively with his fingers. 'You can't keep all this rubbish now you're moving in with Ted. He'll have a fit.'

'No, he won't. If he loves me, he'll love my stuff. That's the way it works.'

'Well, no - it's not the way it works. He can love you to the moon and back and still hate all your stuff. I'd have thought that moving in with your boyfriend would be a good time to clear out and get rid of all this rubbish.'

'Rubbish? Juan - it's not rubbish. I like all these things. They are me...they're part of my history.'

Juan shakes his head as he trudges back inside to collect more of my things. He's muttering under his breath in Spanish. I don't speak his native tongue, but I bet I can translate what he's saying, and it's not very flattering.

He appears a few minutes later with a broken potter's wheel. What can I say? I went to one of those pottery places where you make your own vases, and loved it. So I bought a wheel.

'Really?' he says, walking past me and holding the item aloft. 'I mean - really? A broken wheel thing?'

'I made lovely pots with it. I'll get it mended; then I'll make more pots again.'

'Course you will.'

I can feel Juan's spirit waning. We both started so positively, skipping down the steps with my clothes and kitchen utensils and placing them all gently into the van, but a couple of hours of carrying increasingly daft items while the midday sun blasts us with its rays has dulled the mood somewhat.

'Fancy lunch?' I ask him. 'My treat. We could lock all this in the van, take a walk down to the pub, then come back and finish it all later?'

Juan is easily convinced. He pushes the potters' wheel into the back of the van and tuts when a bit of it falls off.

2

Ten minutes later, we're in the pub garden eating fish and chips (me) and goats cheese salad (him) and drinking cider (a pint for me and a half for him - is it any wonder I'm about twice his weight?).

'I know you think I should have a big clearout, but I don't want to do that. I want to properly share the flat with Ted and not just move in with a handful of things he'll approve of. I want to take it all. It's mine. And I might have things that he doesn't have.'

'Oh, I've no doubt about that. A pottery wheel with a pedal that just fell off, for a start.'

'But it's my pottery wheel with a missing pedal. I like it.'

'I don't think you do, love. If you did, I'd be all for you keeping it. You don't want to throw things away. And, before you say anything, that's different from wanting to keep it.'

'I guess.'

'You're on the 'hoarder' spectrum,' he says.

Oh, I don't like that at all. I give Juan a very stern look.

When I think of hoarders, I think of the weird guy I met

when I went internet dating a while back. Ted and I had split up, so I decided to 'get myself out there.'

I met this one guy whose house was so packed full of stuff you couldn't move around it. You couldn't even use the bathroom because of the detritus in the way. He collected plastic cutlery, among other things. A proper weirdo.

'Do you really think that? I'm not a hoarder, am I? I like having things around me that mean something. Everything in the house doesn't have to be practical and useful. It doesn't even have to be beautiful. It can be packed full of meaning and laden with memories.

'I know, angel. I'm only teasing you. It's just that you are taking a lot of broken things with you, and that seems ever so slightly odd.'

'Ted wouldn't want it any other way,' I lie.

'Are you looking forward to moving to Hampton Court? It's such a very posh place to live.'

It is, indeed. Ted and I have rented a flat on Bridge Road. It's a lovely, quirky part of the world, with lots of independent restaurants and bars, tonnes of antique shops and some lovely, unusual clothes shops with great vintage sections. I can't quite believe I'm going to be living there.

'It will be amazing. You will come around all the time, won't you? I want us to walk down and go into the vintage shops together.'

'I'll be there, don't you worry.'

'And you're coming tomorrow night? For drinks with Charlie and Mike.'

'Of course, I am. It's weird: the two of you are moving in with your boyfriends at the same time. I want to meet this Mike she's shacking up with. What's he like?'

'I don't know. I've not met him.' 'What? Never? You must have.'

'Nope. Not once. I've spoken to him on the phone, and he seems nice...very friendly. And I've seen a picture of him, and he's good-looking, but I've never actually met him.'

'Gosh. Now I'm intrigued to find out what he's like.'

'Me too. They haven't been going out very long, but Charlie is certain he's *the one*.'

'I hope she knows that it's not just her decision. *We* have to decide that he's the one, too.'

'That's exactly what I told her,' I say as I reach over and squeeze Juan's hands. I do love him. He's quite the most wonderful friend.

As we chat, I see a huge platter of food go past us...a grand silver dish loaded with slices of delicious-looking meat, potatoes and piles of vegetables. The waiter lays it down on the table next to us. The table creaks under the weight of it all. I catch the diner's eye.

'Wow. That's a lot of food. Let me know if you need a hand,' I say with a smile.

The diner's face falls. Juan elbows me sharply in the ribs. 'Ow! What did you do that for?'

Juan doesn't speak, but his eyes are wide and staring as if he's trying to tell me something, but he can't bear to let the words out of his mouth.

I look at the man who's just been served his food and gasp in horror. I can feel myself redden.

'Christ, Juan - he's only got one hand.'

'I know.'

'And I said: 'let me know if you need a hand'.'

'I KNOW.'

CHAPTER 3

Sometimes I feel the urge to shout it out loud: I am moving in with Ted.

Can I repeat that: I am moving in with Ted.

It's a particularly wonderful thing to be able to shout, not just because I love him madly, but because there have been occasions on our journey to domestic bliss when any right-thinking person would have bet against us ever being together, let alone moving into a shared flat.

Those who have followed my adventures will know that the path to contentment has been very rocky, with lots of sharp turns, deep dips and the occasional tumble. We've split up, got back together, I've been internet dating, and he went off with someone else. And that's not counting when I stalked him to Amsterdam while dressed in a pink onesie.

So, yes, as I say, it's a miracle we're about to move in together. The place we are moving into isn't any old flat either - I fell in love with it as soon as I saw it. It's the top floor of a 200-year-old former coach house and has two large bedrooms and one smaller one that I'm going to make into a nursery. Joke! No, seriously - that was a joke. It will be an office for Ted so he can work at home a bit more.

The cottage is all white on the outside, with roses growing up next to the front door and inside, there are beams and low ceilings. The place sings and dances with character: it's perfect.

Charlie's place down the road is more modern. She's moving into Mike's house (note - it's a house, not a flat. Mike is loaded). They are next to Hampton Court Palace, just beside the bridge. They have river views. River views! Only celebrities have views of The Thames from their windows.

She's sent me videos, but I can't wait to see it in the flesh, and I can't wait to meet the man she's moving in with. It seems utterly bizarre that none of us has met Mike before, but he's away a lot for work.

He's a high-end jeweller who travels a lot - he travels to Morocco for inspiration and on buying trips to Europe.

I'm not sure what to expect of this guy. In many ways, Mike sounds too good to be true. I don't say that out of any jealousy; I genuinely want Charlie to meet the best person on Earth, but this guy is a craftsman and a businessman all in one (he sells his fantastic artistic jewellery to billionaires, so he is no impoverished, up-and-coming artistic type who is never going to make any money). He seems to adore Charlie: lavishing her with gifts whenever he goes away and sending her love letters galore.

I told Ted about the love letters and gently asked why he's never sent me any notes filled with endearing words.

'I don't think you can trust a man who sends letters in this day and age,' he replied. 'It's not right.'

'It's romantic. Where's your soul?'

'Na. He's a wrong 'un if he's writing her letters. You watch...'

Ted's warning left me more intrigued than ever to meet my best friend's love-letter-writing, expensive-jewellery-creating lover. Luckily...tonight's the night.

Ted and I stride down the road to the Prince of Wales pub where we have planned to meet for drinks.

He swings open the pub door, and I look around excitedly. There's no sign of Charlie and her beau, but Juan is already there, perched on a bar stool, wearing a red beret, a blue and white Breton top and a navy scarf. He's holding his e-cigarette out in front of him between open fingers. He couldn't look more French if he tried.

'Hello, what's the Parisienne get-up all about?' I ask as we kiss on the cheek; he jumps up to shake hands with Ted.

'I watched an interview with Olivier Martinez, the French actor who went out with Kylie Minogue. He looked so gorgeous; I decided I needed to be more French.'

'Well, you certainly look more French.'

'A lot more French than all the men in France,' adds Ted. The new French-style Juan has ordered a bottle of Bordeaux, so we retire to a corner table to await the arrival of Charlie and Mike.

'Do you think we should call them 'Marlie' - you know: Mike and Charlie mixed together?' suggests Juan.

'Or Chike?' I offer.

We've just opted for Marlie when the guest of honour appears, barging through the door and swinging it wide open so it clatters against a table, almost sending a pile of drinks flying. He stands back to allow Charlie through and paces towards us. He's one of those men who looks loud. He hasn't said a word, but you know he dominates zoom meetings, so you can't get a word in edgeways.

I appreciate that I am making a lot of assumptions about

a man I've never even met before but let's be straight here, he's a dickhead. It's clear for everyone to see.

Let me run through his attire for the evening; then, you'll understand the level of dickishness we're talking about here.

He's got trousers on that are too tight, and it's all just a little disturbing. They are so fitted it looks as if the trousers are leaching blood from him to survive. I don't know how he gets them on and off. What I do know is that he doesn't have the legs for them. I bet no one on God's earth has the legs for those. The trousers are also too short – an even bigger sartorial crime as far as I'm concerned. They make his skinny legs look short and scrawny, so they resemble nothing so much as chicken drumsticks.

It also means that you get a fair old chunk of ankle as you look down his legs before your eyes land on Gucci loafers. Of course, he has Gucci loafers. Of course, he does.

I know they are Gucci loafers because they have a big double G on the front. He's exactly the sort of guy who would want everyone to know that he was wearing Gucci loafers, so he would make sure they had the logo on the front...large...in gold.

Mike offers me a big smile while Charlie beams beside him. He's wearing an expensive-looking shirt with cufflinks. To the pub. That's weird behaviour, isn't it? A posh shirt and cuff links to the pub. What's he playing at? Then I spot that the cufflinks have the same double G branding as his shoes.

I have no words.

But Charlie is my best friend, and I should be trying hard to like the guy and get to know him. I shouldn't be so judgemental.

'First impressions?' asks Juan.

'Not keen,' I say.

'But he's handsome,' says Juan. 'You're judging him because he's handsome and well-dressed.'

'I get a bad vibe,' I say, with a knowing shake of my head. 'There's something not right about him. It's the state of the trousers. Has he accidentally put Charlie's trousers on? They don't fit. And all these Gucci cufflinks and matching loafers.'

'And the matching Gucci earring, which I adore,' says Juan.

I look back at Mike, and Juan is right...he's wearing a Gucci earring.

Please give me strength.

'Lovely to meet you, Mary. I've heard so much about you, Mary,' says Mike, shaking my hand while making a spooky amount of eye contact. He should know that there's an appropriate amount of eye contact...too little and you look disengaged; too much, and you look like a serial killer. He's definitely in the serial killer territory.

He also keeps using my name as if I should be thrilled he remembered it. He's been on some negotiating skills course or something where they insist that you address people by their names, so you look genuine.

'So, Mary...' 'Yes, Mary...'

I don't like him. I don't.

While I scowl at Mike, Charlie is waxing lyrical about the house in which she is now living and how incredibly wonderful everything is.

'We get boiling water straight from the tap, no need to wait for the kettle to boil, and he's got these robot vacuums that go round at night and clean up.'

I turn to Juan.

'Why do I hate him so much?' I ask.

'I don't know,' he says. 'I don't understand it. He's come

here, doesn't know anyone and is chatting away. I think he's OK.'

'Nope. He's not OK. He's trouble that one is. Watch my words. He sends her love letters, you know.'

'Well, that's lovely. How charming and old-fashioned. He's gone right up in my estimation.'

'Ted said it was weird that he sent her love letters.'

'Yeah, Ted said that because he's feeling guilty that he never sends you any.'

'Perhaps.'

I look over and see Ted and him exchanging numbers. I feel a cold chill go through me. Ted and he can't be friends. Ted can't wear cropped trousers and Gucci shoes. He'd look ridiculous.

'I'm very successful now, but I was a nightmare at school,' I hear Mike say. 'My whole class once got detention because I drew a penis with a glue stick on the whiteboard, and when the teacher went to wipe off the board, all the fluff came off and stuck to the glue, making it stand out even more.'

Ted laughs rather too heartily at this ridiculous and not-very-funny story.

'I didn't get into trouble,' continues Mike, lifted by the wave of attention. 'I was so popular that none of the kids told the teacher it was me. It pays to be the most popular kid in the class.'

Who talks like that? I mean, who on earth would say that sort of thing?

I can't bear to be part of the Mike Janker appreciation society anymore, so I turn back to Juan.

CHAPTER 4

What's the situation with finding a new flatmate then, my lovely?' I ask Juan. 'Any luck?'

'Oh God, no. I hate it all. I might live by myself.'

'Really?'

'No, not really, but I don't want all the hassle of finding someone. I've got five people coming around tomorrow. Five of them. I bet they all turn out to be lunatics.'

'I'll come round and help,' I offer. 'We can interview them together. It's the least I can do since it's me moving out that has forced you into this position. I'm not working tomorrow.'

'No, you need to concentrate on moving into the new flat. You have to unpack tomorrow,' says Ted. He's listening to our conversation, which speaks volumes for the quality of his conversation with Mike.

'But Juan needs help.'

'Yeah, and we need to get unpacked and moved in,' says Ted.

'Get unpacked, then go and help Juan,' says Mike.

It's a perfectly reasonable suggestion, but I'm determined to ignore it because I don't like Mike.

'No. I'll be round first thing in the morning to help you,' I say to Juan. 'The unpacking and sorting out can wait.'

'She's a very single-minded lady, isn't she?' Says Mike, talking about me to Ted as if I were a small child.

'Indeed,' I say. 'So, tell us a little about yourself, Mike. We don't know much about you at all. Charlie's been keeping you all to herself.'

'You probably know I'm a jeweller to the stars. I've had lots of success professionally. That's why we're in such a beautiful house. You and Ted should come round and...'

'Yes, I know about your job, but what do you do away from work? How long have you lived in the area? What attracted you to our lovely friend.'

'I don't have much time away from work, to be honest. It's all pretty full-on. I like having dinner. I appreciate good food. I like the finer things in life. That's why I'm with Charlie.'

I like that he's flattering Charlie, but I don't like anything else about him. I decide to drink heavily instead. 'Shall I get another bottle of that Bordeaux?' I ask Juan. 'Tonight, I need to drink.'

Ted and I head back that evening, and full of anger and wine, I find myself unable to resist the temptation to tell Ted exactly what I think about the new man in our lives.

'He's a dick,' I conclude, cutting to the chase.

'I thought he was OK.'

'No - he's not. He's trouble. You said he was. You said that writing love letters was a dickish move.'

'Yes, I did say that, sweetheart. But he's your best friend's boyfriend, and they've just moved in together, so I think we'll have to learn to get along with him.'

There's no reply to that sort of logic. Since when did Ted start getting all sensible? I'm sure there was a time when I could offer an irrational dislike of someone, and he'd nod in agreement and confirm that only seriously ill-adjusted people wore Gucci earrings. Not tonight.

In the early hours of the morning, I'm woken up by a sudden noise. It's a bell ringing so loudly that I'm thrown out of my dream. I open my eyes and feel crushed by panic. I'm in a cold sweat, shaking and gasping for breath.

I sit up, holding my head in my hands. It's the doorbell ringing, I'm sure of it.

Ted sits up next to me. 'What's the matter?'

'The doorbell. Someone's ringing the doorbell. At 4am. I bet it's Mike.'

'What?' says Ted. 'Why the hell would Mike turn up and ring the doorbell?'

'I don't know, but a man wearing trousers like that is capable of literally anything. You'll have to go down there and find out. Take a knife. The man's probably a serial killer.'

Ted hurls himself out of bed, shaking his head at me, and paces towards the bedroom door. He begins to head down the stairs. UNARMED. What's he doing? Mike probably has a machine gun.

This is going to be like Peaky Blinders. I slink back under the covers.

I hear Ted open the door. Oh, God. Why did Charlie have to choose a mass murderer to go out with?

I hear the door close and Ted walking back up the stairs. At least, I hope it's Ted. Perhaps Mike has murdered Ted and is coming up the stairs to murder me. Oh, Christ alive.

Then the unmistakable figure of Ted appears in the doorway.

'Babe?' he says.
'Yes?' I reply, with a shaky voice.
'It wasn't our doorbell.'
'It was,' I insist. 'I heard it.'
'Nope. It wasn't,' says Ted.
'How do you know that?'
'We don't have a fucking doorbell.'

CHAPTER 5

Juan and I sit in his flat, my old flat, waiting for the succession of would-be flatmates to arrive and persuade us that they're not lunatics or kleptomaniacs.

'We're going to find you someone lovely and amazing to live with today, so don't you worry about a thing, my little angel,' I say, patting Juan's leg.

'Why are you talking to me as if I'm six?'

'I don't know. I'm just all tired and angry after last night.'

'I can tell.'

'I don't trust Mike, and I don't know why. Then I couldn't sleep because I was having nightmares about him ringing the doorbell at 4 am.'

'What?'

'Yep. I made Ted go and answer the door.'

'And was he there?'

'No - of course, he wasn't. I'm completely losing my mind.'

'I thought he was alright, Mary. Honestly. He's a bit flashy. He thinks a lot of himself, but that's OK. And he's very talented. Have you seen his website? All the amazing jewellery he creates? He's a real artist.'

'Yeah, I've seen his website. Very pretentious.'

'Very beautifully crafted, you mean. There were these bangles with sapphires dripping off them like they were flowing down the model's arm. They were so incredibly beautiful they stopped me in my tracks. They were called waterfall bangles, and they were £100k each. They also had ones with rubies - they were called fire, and the diamond ones were called 'ice.'

'Did you buy me one?'

'I bought you one of each.'

'It's not going to work, you know.'

'What isn't?'

'Charlie and Mike, the artistic jewellery designer. He's a dick, and she's lovely; they are unsuited.'

'Give them a chance, love. They've only just moved in together.'

'Yeah, I know. I'll try to stop going about it, but it's very distracting when your friend's going out with a horror story.'

'Well, you can't be distracted this morning because you've got to help me spot the person who will be perfect for me to live with. You can't be in a frenzy about Charlie's love life, or you might accidentally encourage me to live with someone who cuts my toes off one by one at night.'

'Don't worry; I can spot a toe snipper at 100 paces. Now, who's first?'

'A guy called Dale is coming at 10.30 am. He's the least impressive sounding of all of them, so he's first. I promise you; they will get better after that.'

'Oh lord. Why did you invite him if he isn't very impressive sounding?'

'I don't know. I thought it was worth having a few candidates. And you can't tell what people are like until you meet them.'

'No, that's true. Let me have his CV.'

'CV? Was I supposed to get CVs from them?'

'Well, yes. If not a CV, then a letter of recommendation, a letter from a referee, or some information about them. They must have sent in some information about themselves when they said they wanted to live with you, didn't they?'

'No, they didn't apply or anything. I just rang them because they all put notes on Facebook last week, saying they were looking for somewhere to live. I invited them for interviews.'

'But they might not be whom they say they are. We might have a whole load of complete nutters coming in today.'

'There's every chance. I don't know. We'll find out.'

At 10.20 am, Dale arrives at the door, and as Juan predicted, he is unimpressive. I mean - it's not as if we are trying to recruit a nuclear scientist, but we are looking for someone who can hold a conversation and doesn't look as if he might dress as a zombie and paint the windows black in the dark of the night. I couldn't make that promise about Dale. He comes shuffling into the house, looking down at the carpet. It is all I could do not to shout, 'pick your feet up' and 'lift your head and look at us while you're talking to us.'

He doesn't put his hand out to shake hands, so when I put mine out, it is left hanging and I am forced to pull it back in again.

'What sort of things do you like doing?' I ask.

'Nothing,' he replies.

'No hobbies or anything like that? Do you enjoy watching films or going to the gym or anything?'

'I'm obsessed with gaming,' he says.

I know nothing about gaming, and I don't mean to be rude or disrespectful to any gamers out there, but I thought straight away, 'ah...that makes sense. The pasty complexion and the inability to make eye contact with a human being - are all characteristics of a guy obsessed with gaming.'

Dale would be your first call if you had to find someone who looked like a gamer to star in an ad or something.

'When the new *Call of Duty* game comes out, I disappear for days to play,' he says. 'I don't take toilet breaks or anything. I keep going - playing through the night to get as far along in the game as I can.'

'Sorry? No toilet breaks?'

'You can't take toilet breaks; you can't let your eyes move from the screen. You have to be full-on concentrating. I've got two screens, one for each eye.'

'One for each eye?' says Juan. 'I don't think it works like that. Your eyes don't separate and look at different things.'

'Yes, mine do; I've trained them to do that.'

'Can I take you back to something you said earlier,' I say. I can't let this go. I really can't. 'You said you don't take toilet breaks. Does that mean you starve yourself or something, or don't eat and drink for days?

'Ha ha. That's where I get one up on the other players. Because I have a secret.'

'Go on...'

'Adult nappies,' he says.

I swear this is true; the man looks me in the eye and tells me that he wears adult nappies all night while playing games in his room. I glance at Juan, and the look of horror and dismay on the man's face will stay with me for a long time. He looks like a dead fish - mouth wide, eyes staring ahead with an emptiness that tells of his dismay with the whole of humanity.

'You know you just said that out loud, don't you?' says Juan, mouthing the words slowly and carefully. 'I mean - you're in an interview to become my flatmate, and you say that out loud. So that we can hear it.'

I nod as Juan speaks. Who in their right mind would put adult nappies on to avoid going to the toilet first? But who would then announce that in an interview for a flatshare?

'You can go now,' says Juan.

'We'll be in touch,' I say as he stands up and shuffles his way out of the flat.

'Really?' I say to Juan. 'Have you lost your mind? How could you have even invited someone like that into the flat, let alone considered living with them? You are bonkers.'

'I didn't know he was mad. How was I supposed to know he wore adult nappies? And don't tell me that I should have asked him to send me his CV because he wouldn't have written that in a CV, would he?'

I laugh at this point.

'But wouldn't it have been funny if he had? 'I acquire professional advantage from wearing adult nappies. These allow me to keep playing through the night without interruption.'

Juan laughs too. 'Please find a picture attached of me in my adult nappies.'

'Hopefully, the others will be better...'

'Well, yes. They can't be much worse, can they? I mean, all they have to do is use the toilet, and they will instantly be an improvement.'

CHAPTER 6

When the next interviewee arrives, I'm still shaking my head at the idea of a grown man sitting in his room, pooing into nappies all night. His name is Brendan, and he seems much better: smart, smiley and handsome. I'd wager that this one has no problems going to the bathroom at night. He's also handsome. Did I mention that?

'Oo la la,' says Juan, and he's not wrong. Brendan is very *oo la la* indeed.

'Take a seat,' I say.

Brendan spins the chair around in an utterly fabulous fashion and sort of slides onto it without losing eye contact, as if he's in a Hollywood musical.

'Tell us a bit about yourself.'

'My name is Brendan,' he confirms. 'I'm 24 years old and have a degree in art. I love sculpture, and I'm very into conceptual art.'

I nod knowingly, without having the slightest clue what conceptual art is. I suspect it's the art that isn't art at all...you know - just an ashtray lying there to show the impoverished nature of human existence or a single balloon to illustrate the ephemeral nature of life.

'I love galleries and hope to own a gallery one day, showing my art.

He smells strongly of smoke. I suspect he's on about 40 a day, given the strong aroma emanating from him.

'Having your own gallery would be incredible. Have you managed to sell much of your art so far?'

'It's not all about selling. It's about the glory of creating. Van Gogh never sold a piece of art while he was alive. I think we can become too fixated on the process of selling. We should never let economic forces come between us and creativity.'

Naturally, I agree with him entirely, but I'm nervous about Juan's rent payments.

'So, are you confident you'll be able to pay the rent?' I ask cautiously.

'It may be hard some months, but I'll always try. When I can't produce actual money, I will always be able to produce art that, in many ways, is worth much more than money. In my last accommodation, I made a man completely out of newspaper, dressed him in a suit and sat him at the table. He represented the callousness of modern media.'

'That sounds interesting, but we do need a guarantee that you will be able to pay the rent,' I say, though I can see that Juan looks quite taken with the idea of newspapermen sitting around the table.

'There's no way I can give you a guarantee. That's an insane thing to ask an artist. How can I possibly make a guarantee like that? You are not an artist, are you?'

'Nope. I'm not an artist at all. I work very hard in a DIY shop. I don't love it, and there are days when I wouldn't say I like it, but I do it to pay the rent. That's kind of how it works in the real world.'

'Do you have any work you're developing now?' asks Juan. He's taken a fancy to this artist and hopes the man will convince us that he can earn money to pay the rent.

'My project at the moment is difficult to sell. It's a rebellion against the comforts of domestic life. We've been filming today and hope to be able to edit it and put it online in the next few weeks or whenever the muse comes again. It's impossible to say when.'

'A rebellion against the comforts of domestic life? That sounds interesting. What will the video be about?'

'It's me setting fire to a carpet. I have three carpet squares, and I throw petrol on them and burn them. There is fire; then there is smoke. It is significant. The smoke means something.'

'Well, the smoke means there's been a fire.'

Brendan glances sideways at me as if I'm a lesser being who doesn't understand the purity and beauty of art.

'You will call me to let me know when I can move in?' he says.

'We'll call you and let you know whether you are moving in here,' I explain.

He walks away. He's been setting fire to carpets. That's why he smells of bloody smoke.

'He seemed OK,' says Juan, watching him leave. 'Let's offer him the room.'

'No, Juan,' I say. 'He's never going to pay you a penny in rent. It would be a disaster if he moved in.' Thank God I'm here.

I don't want to bore you with the details about Norman and Alistair who came next, both of whom were OK. They'd be able to pay the rent and wouldn't set fire to the carpets, but they would never cope with Juan's mad outbursts and lunatic outfits.

They were both too narrow-minded, too unworldly. I'm Juan's biggest fan, but let's be honest - he's a total nutter, and they will come home one day to find him practising pilates in a tutu or doing yoga in the shower. I don't think Norman and Alistair would be able to cope.

I was starting to think that the day was a write-off, and if I weren't careful, Juan would have to move in with Ted and me when Andrew arrived. Lovely, lovely Andrew.

CHAPTER 7

Andrew walks into the room for his interview, and it's a revelation. Juan and I can see immediately that he is normal and fun. He is just like us: he works hard, wants to have a laugh, doesn't take himself too seriously and comes with references from previous landlords despite Juan not asking for references of any kind.

'He's the one,' I whisper to Juan as Andrew chats about his membership at the gym and how he never went there last year but used the car park once, so he thinks he might have the most expensive car park in the whole of London. He talks about going out with friends, the girl at work called Daisy, who he fancies but hasn't got the guts to do anything about. He's great.

Juan smiles. 'I can relax with him. He's nice,' he says.

'Yep - sign him up. Call off the search. Ring the others and tell them they haven't been selected.'

'I hate to tell people they haven't been selected,' says Juan, looking downbeat at the thought.'

'I'll do it,' I say. Then I think of the mad artist and nappy boy.

'I'll text them later and tell them there's been a change of plan or something.'

'Yes,' says Juan. 'And we will tell Andrew he can move in straight away.'

'Yes,' I say. 'You want him to move in next week, do you?'

'Or tonight. I hate being here by myself. The flat is too big for one person. I can hear the walls talking to me.'

'You nutcase. Come and stay at ours tonight, and we'll phone Andrew and tell him he's free to move in on Tuesday.'

'I can't stay with you in your new flat on your first night there. Ted will be furious.'

'Ted is never furious. He won't mind a bit, you nutter. We've got a spare room. I mean, it's full of boxes and all sorts of rubbish, but it's spare.'

'Is the potter's wheel in there?'

'You know - I think it is.'

'What about the oboe.'

'Yep.'

'Great. I'm in.'

It's late by the time Ted gets back, and Juan and I are on our second bottle. We're tipsy but not drunk - just very smiley, happy and silly and thrilled that Juan has a nice flatmate, despite nappy-gate and the fire-starting artist.

Ted thunders in and stands there with his hands on his hips. His tie is askew, and he looks hot and bothered from the train and bus. No one should be made to go by public transport in this weather. It's against the Geneva Convention, surely.

'Everything OK?' I ask.

'No. I'm a dick,' he says. 'I'm the biggest dick who ever lived.'

'No, really love - you're not. We met a man who wears adult nappies today; you're not even close to being the biggest dick.'

'Yeah - well, I'm right up there. Definitely in the top three. What do you mean - adult nappies?'

'It's a long story, love. Carry on.'

'Do you remember Steve Morgan? The guy I used to play rugby with?'

'Yes, of course, I do. He's good fun. I like him a lot.'

'Yeah, well, we used to have this thing on the coach when we were travelling away to matches - if one of us saw a vacant seat, he would rush to it and push the other one out of the way to get to it. The one who didn't get the seat would have to sit on the other one's lap the whole way to the match without saying anything. Just silly rugby stuff. You know what we're all like.'

I nod at this. I've heard enough of Ted's rugby stories to understand that they are all bonkers.

'Well, I saw Steve on the bus today. He was standing there, reading the newspaper. I walked up to say hello, just as the girl sitting next to where he was standing got up and left the bus. Steve went to sit down, and I thought - I really can't miss this opportunity - so I switched up a gear, dived in, grabbed him, threw him out of the way and sat down.

'You have to sit on my lap, you old dog,' I said.'

'Ha. ha. That's fun. What did Steve say?'

'Yeah, well, that was the problem. It turned out it wasn't Steve. It was someone who looked a lot like him. Like I said: I'm a dick.'

CHAPTER 8

'What do you think of our new flat, then?' I ask Juan as we're lying on the sofas the next morning, laughing at the story Ted told last night and contemplating whether that's the weirdest thing ever to happen to someone on the R68 bus.

'I love it,' he says. 'I was so sad when you said you were moving out, but this place is perfect for the two of you. And it's just down the road from Charlie. Honestly, I'm so pleased for you both. This is a special time, my angel, and you deserve it. After all you and Ted have been through, I'm so glad you are in this position.'

'Thank you. I don't know how I'd have coped without you these past few years. You've kept me sane.'

'Not many people tell me I keep them sane, so thank you.'

'No - you definitely did. Do you remember when you bombed out to Italy to comfort me when I'd heard that Ted was going out with horrible Dawn?'

'Oh blimey, yes. Of course, I do.'

'And the fitness guy fancied you. That was funny.'

'Yeah, that bit wasn't so funny. His fiancee certainly didn't see the funny side at all.'

'You are lovely, Juan. You're welcome here anytime you want. That bedroom there is all yours.'

'Thank you, darling. You are so kind. This place is gorgeous, and the area is stunning. I want to explore all those antique shops. This road is the most fabulous ever. It's a boutique-filled heaven. We need to go down and have a good look. I've only peered through the windows; I've never been in there.'

'Shall we go now? We can have a look around the shops and have some breakfast.'

'Oh yes, darling. That would be fab.'

Finding my trainers beneath the avalanche of boxes, books, and clothes piled up in our bedroom takes quite a while. I sit back onto a book about mushrooms to do them up. I swear to God, I don't know where half this stuff originated. Why would I ever have bought a book about mushrooms?

'Let's go,' I say, scrambling to my feet and heading for the door. Juan follows me out.

'I've just realised; you've got no doorbell,' he remarks.

'I know. Ted discovered that in the early hours of the morning when I sent him out to check whether Mike was ringing the doorbell. We realised he wasn't ringing it because I don't have a doorbell.'

'Darling, Mike wouldn't be ringing your doorbell early in the morning because he's not a nutter.'

'I wouldn't go that far. I mean, those trousers. Did you see them? They were more fitted than a ballet dancer's tights.'

We walk down the road towards the string of antique shops that sit in the middle of the pretty road that I now call home. Further from the antique shops are lots of lovely bars and restaurants, and just past them is Charlie's place.

'Oh. My. God!' shrieks Juan. 'Have you ever seen anything so incredibly beautiful...'

He's looking into the window of one of the shops like a lover from a Shakespeare play, staring longingly at the pretty girl he wishes to marry. 'I have to have it,' he says. 'Whatever else happens in my life, I must have this.'

I stand next to him and peer through the glass. There's a ridiculously huge pair of antlers at the top of the display; then there's an old painting easel with splashes of colour on it. Does he mean that? Or the beautiful brass planter with elegant handles on the side? There are mirrors, a small cabinet, a monkey on a pole with a light in its mouth, and a lovely collection of silver elephants.

'What are you looking at?' I ask.

'The antlers,' he says in an emotion-packed whisper. 'It's the antlers.'

'Really?'

'Yes. They're amazing.'

'Are they?' I ask. 'I mean - aren't they horrible? Some poor stag's been shot and had his antlers removed. I don't get how that's amazing.'

But Juan's not listening. He's walking towards the shop door while still staring at the antlers in the window in something of a trance.

I stay outside on the pavement and watch him go in and chat with the man in the shop. They converse for a while then he stands back while the shop owner and another guy attempt to take the antlers down. The guys can't manage to move them on their own, so another man goes over. It takes three strapping men to get them down and carry them over to Juan. How in the name of the lord does he think we're going to be able to get them home?

He signals for me to come into the shop. I swear to God, he's insane. You know everything that I was saying about him being a great friend? Well, I take it all back. Every last word. He's a complete liability.

'I'm going to need some help with these,' he says as I stand next to him and look down at the enormous antlers in front of us. 'These beauties are heavier than they look. It's definitely not a one-man job.'

'No, indeed,' I say, as I look at the three men who were needed to move the enormous things just a couple of feet. 'It might not be a two-person job either.'

'Yeah, we can do it,' he insists, taking his credit card and a receipt from the manager and walking behind the men as they carry his new interior decoration outside.

'How much did you pay?' I ask, but Juan pretends he can't hear me.

'I'm guessing it was a lot, then.'

'I paid what they're worth,' he says, bending down to kiss the antlers that the guys have now laid on the floor.

'I don't know how we're going to get them to your place, Juan. Perhaps we should take them to mine and drive them over when Ted gets back from work?'

But Juan's not listening. A huge bald eagle on a plinth now transfixes him. The eagle's wings are outstretched as if he were preparing for flight.

'Look at that beauty...'

'No,' I say sternly as if talking to a dog. 'I'm not carrying a 6ft bald eagle back, as well as the enormous antlers.'

'OK, OK,' he says. 'Just the antlers for now, then.'

'How are we going to carry these?' I say.

'They're beautiful,' he replies. 'Look at them - just beautiful.'

'Yeah, well, we might have to disagree on that one, but we need to agree on the way to carry them.'

'We'll lift them. We can do it,' says Juan.

So, that's what we do. We lift the monstrous things and stagger off with them, bumping into people on the narrow shopping street and causing children to stop and stare.

'I've been living here for a day, and I'm causing a scene,' I say to Juan. 'The people around here are sophisticated. I can't go embarrassing myself like this.'

'Come on, let's just get to the corner, by the butchers, and we'll take a break,' he says.

We stagger on until we reach the appointed stopping place and drop the antlers with a thud. I move to stand up properly and feel my whole back creak in discomfort. As soon as I get myself fully upright, Juan signals for me to pick the things back up again. Luckily, the sound of my phone ringing bursts from my handbag.

'I'll just get this,' I tell him.

I open the phone case, and Charlie's face flashes up on the screen. It always makes me laugh when she calls because I have a picture of her taken at a party many years ago, in which she has her face painted like a cat but has run her hand all over it and ruined it. And it looks like she's emerged from a day shift as a coal miner.

'How are you doing, my lovely? Juan has just bought the biggest set of antlers. You should have seen us trying to manoeuvre them down the street. At least he didn't buy the bald eagle, though. We're not far from your house. Do you want to come out and meet us?'

There's silence on the other end.

'We're near the butcher's.'

Silence again.

Then I hear sniffling, a gasp for breath, and a snorty sound like she's trying to stop herself from crying. Then a torrent of tears. She tries to explain to me, between the gasps for breath and the cries and wails, exactly what happened.

'A box of letters and photos. So young. The girl is so young.'

'Charlie, what is it? What's happened?'

'He's a bastard. Why does this always happen to me? Why?'

'Why does *what* always happen to you?'

'I found a box,' she says, in a shaky voice, still gasping and snorting. 'Well, it's a sort of tin. It has 'confessions' printed on it.'

Then there are more tears.

'Look, do you want us to come around?' I ask.

'Yes,' she says. 'Yes. Can you come straight away?'

'Of course,' I reply. 'We'll be there in five minutes.'

I tuck the phone back into my bag and look at Juan: 'We need to go to Charlie's straightaway. She's really upset. Something's happened; I don't know what. But she's crying and moaning, and she's found a tin or something. She sounds like she's in a bad way.'

'Come on then, let's go,' he says.

We bend down to pick up the antlers and head off down the street in the direction of my sad friend, but it's proving extremely difficult to carry them at waist height. We're filling up the whole pavement and struggling to walk as they bang against our legs.

'I've got an idea,' says Juan. 'We need to hold them as the deer holds them.'

'That's ridiculous,' I say. 'We'll be the laughing stock of

Hampton Court.'

'Any better ideas?' he asks as the edge of one of the antlers bashes against a lady's buggy.

'No,' I reply, and the two of us lift the set of extraordinarily large antlers skywards and rest them on our shoulders.

Actually, it turns out that it is easier to hold them higher up, though we look like we've escaped some mental institution.

We stagger towards Charlie's house, proudly holding antlers above our heads like wild stags.

We arrive and knock on the door, waiting patiently for her to answer with the antlers still on our shoulders. Charlie answers the door in complete distress...tears, anguish and sadness are written all over her face.

She stands and looks at us, and suddenly the fact that we've arrived with giant antlers on our shoulders seems monstrously inappropriate.

Then she starts crying again and looks so small and vulnerable that I desperately want to hug her.

'Can you take them?' I say to Juan, moving from under the bony horns and stepping towards Charlie to wrap her up in a huge cuddle. But, of course, Juan can't hold them on his own. There's a loud groan as his knees buckle under the weight he's now carrying, but I'm too fixated on Charlie's sad face to notice.

'What's the matter?' I ask her. Charlie is also unaware of the commotion in the background: a man carrying a large set of antlers crashing to the ground, cries from passers-by, a car horn, and then people running over to help.

'It's Mike,' says Charlie. 'I think he's having an affair.'

'Oh angel, no - he can't be. You've just moved in together; that's impossible,' I say.

'I think he is. And why is Juan lying in the street? And what's he carrying? Has he been in a fight with a deer?'

'Really, it's nothing. You go in, I'll help Juan to his feet, and we'll follow you in two minutes and sort all this out.'

'OK,' says Charlie softly, glancing from me to Juan before shaking her head and walking inside.

'What are you doing?' I say to my prone friend.

'I could ask you the same thing of you, darling. You let go of the bloody antlers. I had all the weight.'

'I had to. Charlie was sad. Come on, up you get.'

A small crowd has gathered, and a few phones are pulled out so pictures can be taken of this rather unlikely tableau.

Then, finally, some kindness.

'Can I help?' A rather attractive man in an unattractive orange coat steps forward. Then others do, too, until there are around six of us lifting the antlers to reveal a rather distraught-looking Juan in a crumpled heap beneath them.

He stands and tries to style it out by acting as if it is natural for man to find himself in such a predicament. Then he moves casually to one side while we hold them, wondering what the next move is.

'We need to get them into the house,' I say. I know Charlie needs me and is probably wondering why it is taking me so long to make the short journey from the front door to the sitting room.

The trouble is that getting a large set of antlers through a normal-sized door is very hard. Have you ever tried? No - forget that question - of course, you haven't.

Well, I'll tell you, it's not easy. In the end, while Charlie sits on the sofa, sobbing her little heart out, three strangers and I push the antlers through the sitting room window until they plonk onto the sofa next to her and then drop onto the carpet. I swear, she doesn't even look up.

I thank the kind strangers and join Charlie on the sofa. 'What's the matter, angel?' I ask.

Charlie is staring at the antlers lying on the floor; she seems slightly mesmerised by the spikes and curls of horn dominating her sitting room. Juan joins us on the sofa, and we sit with our arms around one another in solidarity while a set of extraordinarily large antlers look up at us from the floor.

'He's having an affair,' she stutters.

'I'm sure he's not, angel,' I say, though it does seem eminently likely that he's having affairs. He seems the type. But, as you know, I'm biased. I saw the trouser situation - it's impossible not to be biased after that.

'He is sending letters to his other girlfriend…it's all here.'

She indicates the box next to her. It's an aged metal tin with 'Confessions' written on the front, which strikes me as incredibly obvious. If you are going to betray someone, do you put the evidence in a box marked 'Confessions?' I'm sure that if he just used an old cornflake box or something, she'd never have found it. He's stupid as well as being a sartorially-challenged two-timer.

The picture on the lid is of a large and rather delicious-looking ice cream, indicating that the tin once held a frosty dessert called 'confessions.' I find my mind wandering. I fancy a confessions ice cream dessert right now.

'You haven't known him long…perhaps he's just writing to an old friend?' tries Juan.

Charlie shrugs. She's unconvinced.

'It could be, though. Please don't jump to conclusions and write him off.'

'Yeah, sure, could be,' she says, with little conviction.

'Lots of friends send you love letters telling you they adore you.'

Charlie eases open the lid of the box, and it makes a strange sound...like sandpaper rubbing against metal. The tin is all rusty. It looks as if it's from the 1950s or something. She pulls out a photo.

'Look...'

There is a picture of her boyfriend with a young woman.

Too young. The girl in the picture can't be more than 19 or 20. I notice that Mike is wearing his Gucci loafers in the picture and is grinning in a smarmy way.

'His daughter?' tries Juan.

'He's only 32; how could she be his daughter? It says 'love Lola' on the back. She must be a girlfriend. This is just awful. This photo was taken recently because he's wearing those lovely shoes and he only bought them two weeks ago. AFTER he'd asked me to move in with him.'

'It could be a client. She's wearing a necklace in the picture...perhaps she's grateful to him for the lovely piece of jewellery that he made.'

'No, it's not right. That's not the sort of jewellery he makes. And look at these...'

Charlie hands us another picture of Mike and Lola together. In this one, he's lifting her into the air, and they are smiling at one another like lovers. There's no getting away from it...they look like two people in love.

'She's so young,' Charlie keeps muttering.

Lola does indeed look young but not particularly attractive. She's very thin, with long mousey straight brown hair. She's quite pale and bland. She's the sort of person you'd walk past in the street without even noticing.

'She's nothing to look at.' I say. 'She doesn't seem like the sort of girl he'd go after, especially when he has you.'

In contrast to Lola's pale, insignificant looks, Charlie is a tanned, blonde bombshell with a beautiful figure (she is size eight and gets very upset if she has to go up to a size 10. Witch!). Charlie has beautiful big blue eyes. You can't even see Lola's eyes in the photo; they are so narrow.

I turn the picture over, and it says, 'All my love, Lola xx.'

Then I spot something else as well.

'There's a phone number on the back of this one,' I say, realising as I utter the words that I might be playing with fire.'

'Let's bloody ring her,' says Charlie. 'I'll just ask her what the hell's going on.'

'OK, that's certainly a possibility, or you could talk to Mike and ask him?'

'He'll lie,' she says. 'Who could believe a word he says after all this?'

Charlie then pulls out what she describes as 'further pieces of damning evidence' and holds them aloft, like Judge Rinder.

I take the letters from her and start to read them. They are full of warmth and love, saying how much the writer misses Mike.

Lola's obviously in love with the man.

Hang on.

'These letters are signed 'Anna',' I say. 'The photo has a message on the back from Lola, but these are signed by Anna, and the handwriting is completely different. These are two different people.'

'No, it's the same person,' says Charlie confidently. 'The handwriting is not that different. I think 'Lola' must be his special nickname for her.'

I don't say anything, but I think the handwriting is very different. I hug Charlie closely and let her cry on my shoulder. She wails and utters half-sentences. The tears are flowing so freely that my shoulder is wet.

Juan picks up the letters in a manly, authoritative way and starts reading through them.

'The first thing you need to do is talk to him. Ask him to explain,' he says.

'But then he'll know that I've been snooping.'

'Can't you say you stumbled upon it?'

'It was hidden away.'

'Tell him you were doing a deep clean.'

'He won't be back for a few days because they have a Scottish launch of the new necklace lines. He's staying in Edinburgh.'

'Phone him?' suggests Juan, leaning over to give Charlie a huge hug but snagging his shin on the spiky bone of the antler in the process.

He swears and clutches his leg while Charlie reaches for the remote control and turns on the tv. She doesn't answer Juan. Instead, she stares, transfixed, at the wave of perfect-looking people washing across the screen.

'I'd rather not talk about it,' she says. 'Let's watch this. I taped it last night.'

'Oh, OK,' says Juan, startled at the sudden switch in conversation. 'I didn't mean to upset you.'

'No, you didn't. I'm just a bit cried out. I love you two so much,' says Charlie. 'I'm so glad I have you in my life.'

We all hug at this stage. It's a bit awkward, what with the antlers to negotiate, but we manage it.

'Now, come on, let's watch....'

I switch my attention from the horrible two-timer to the bikini bodies in front of me.

'What are we watching?' I ask.

'Love Island. I taped it last night.'

I rarely watch such things, being a woman of great intellect and sophistication (!), but I slump next to her on the sofa and watch the television, swearing, judging, and loathing.

'This programme is appalling. It's all oily men and women with their bums hanging out,' I say.

'No, it's great. I find it very distracting,' says Chalie.

Once she's said that, I realise we'll have to carry on watching it. I can't make her switch it off and risk her bursting into tears again, can I?

Then, something rather terrible happens...I start to like it. I fall in love with Roddy and Mel and hope they leave their respective partners and get together. Conversely, I build up such a repository of dislike for Chantilly that I am close to blaming her for everything bad in the world. I'm certainly close to blaming her for Mike being unfaithful. At the end of the show, they dump someone off the island, and I have my head in my hands, praying it's not MelRod. I give out a cackle of joy when Chantilly's name is picked.

'I thought you didn't like Love Island,' says Charlie.

'Turns out I do like it. When's the next episode?'

'Tonight,' says Charlie with a smile. 'It's on every night.'

'Oh,' I say, smiling back at her. 'Do you want to come and stay at mine tonight, and we can watch it together?'

'What about me?' says Juan. 'Can I come, too?'

'Of course you can. But you have to cheer for Roddy and Mel.'

'You know what I keep thinking,' says Charlie. 'Where is Anna now, then? Why isn't she here on the squishy sofas if she's so wonderful? Why hasn't she moved in with him? And where's Lola? Why's he living here with me if those two slags are so important to him?'

'Only Mike can answer that, sweetie,' says Juan gently.

'I know, and I will call him. But he'll be furious that I looked through all his things. I probably shouldn't have looked, but I couldn't help it.'

CHAPTER 9

Charlie is reflecting on the fact that she went looking through all of Mike's things. She keeps saying how bad she feels. 'Have you looked through Ted's belongings since you moved in with him?' she asks. 'Or is it just me who does that sort of thing?'

'Of course, I have, love. I went rifling through his things in the manner of a deranged FBI agent looking for clues about a missing child.'

They both laugh at this, which cheers me.

'And you found nothing?'

'Nothing at all.'

'I wish I'd found nothing at all. Who do you think this Anna is? And why are there letters from her in my boyfriend's wardrobe? And what are the pictures of Lola all about?'

This is the difficult thing about going through someone's private affairs...there is the thrill, and the excitement at what you might discover that precedes any search, but this soon descends into horror and regret when you do discover something.

Added to that is the fact that you know nothing about the context of the discovery or what it really means, so it hits you like a sledgehammer

'Listen to this,' says Charlie, reading out from the back of the photo of Lola.

'MY DARLING MIKE, I miss you so much, I want to be with you always and forever. The words you sent to me mean so much, thank you for being in my life. Lola.'

Charlie drops the letter onto the sofa, and Juan promptly picks it up.

'Even if this was sent a long time ago, it's annoying that he's still kept it. You're going to have to ask him why.'

'None of the letters or photos were sent a long time ago. That's what I'm saying - these photos were taken in the last two weeks, and the letters are dated in the last few weeks. The confessions box is full of recent correspondence with his ladies. If I looked properly, I'd probably find loads more letters here.'

'No, no, no,' says Juan. 'You must not go searching for anything else. First, you have to talk to him.'

'I don't know how to do that. What will I ask?'

Between every word that Charlie says, there's a splutter, a snort, a sniff and a whine like a puppy who's had its paw stepped on.

'This is what you need to ask,' says Juan. 'Go and get a notebook.'

Charlie slouches off and returns with a few bits of paper.

'I can't find a notebook. I can't find anything. This is chaos. I haven't even unpacked, and now I probably don't need to.'

Then tears come again - horrible, snotty, snorty tears that leave her shaking in their wake.

'Write this down...'

'I haven't got a pen,' she says.

'For the love of God...'

'You didn't tell me to get a pen.'

Juan hands her his favourite biro, and she takes it ungraciously and looks down at the badly ripped bits of paper on her lap.

'This is like my life,' she wails. 'I haven't even got a pen, and this paper's all tatty and ripped.'

I can see Juan tiring of the whole routine.

'I want to help you, lovely. Write these questions down now, and stop snorting.'

His abruptness takes Charlie back. 'OK,' she mutters.

'You need to find out: Who is she? Where is she now? When did they see each other? Why is she writing to him? Does she live a long way from him? That'll do for starters. Now try calling him again.'

'I will...later.'

'Why do it later? Just call me now.'

'He's busy,'

'Then leave him a message asking him to call you when he's not busy.'

There's silence from our tearful friend.

'You'll never be able to have a meaningful relationship with him with this hanging over you.'

'I know. But what if there's a straightforward explanation? Then he'll explain it all, and I'll be left looking like a lunatic stalker for going through all his stuff.'

I take her point. I mean - none of us wants to look like a crazy lunatic.

'I need to find out about the woman in the letters without talking to Mike,' she concludes.

'Then you'll need to get hold of his phone and start trawling through his messages. If you can't get your hands on his phone, you're going to have to access his emails and phone messages from your phone,' says Juan, way too quickly, so quickly that he could easily be mistaken for a guy who's done this sort of thing before.

'You want her to tap into his phone? Did you work for the *News of the World* in the 90s by any chance?'

'I'm just trying to help,' he says.

'Or you could try googling the women to see whether you can find out more.'

I pull out my phone and call up the mighty google in an attempt to find out anything I can about Lola and Anna, but we don't have enough basic information about either of them. We know that Anna's surname is Day, but there are lots of Anna Days...it's impossible to work out which one is ours. The name Lola is less common, but we don't have a surname. It's hopeless.

'Perhaps Juan's right, and we do have to resort to underhand tactics. Shall we employ a private detective firm?'

'I didn't mean going quite that far,' says Juan. 'It's just that lots of people have their phones set up so they can access messages remotely. Perhaps he does, and perhaps we can tap into them and listen in.'

'I wouldn't have a clue how he accesses his messages,' says Charlie. She doesn't look impressed with Juan's suggestion. 'I don't really want to do that, to be honest.'

'OK, just trying to help. If you don't want to talk to him or look in his phone, and there's nothing on google, how can you possibly find out more?'

'By talking to her?'

'Her? Who?'

'Lola - the woman whose number is in the letters, and Anna whose address is on the letter.'

I reach down and pick up the letter from Anna, and -

sure enough - her address is on the top of it. She lives in Oxford.

'Are you suggesting that we go to Oxford on a mission to find out?'

'That's exactly what I'm suggesting,' she says. 'Are you coming?'

'Yes!' I say, without really thinking through the consequences. 'We'll go on an undercover mission.'

'Is this wise,' says Juan, but it's too late; I'm overtaken by the excitement of it all.

'I'll bring disguises: false beards and wigs and things so that we can go undetected through the streets of Oxford.'

'Oh dear lord,' says Juan. 'Dear lord, dear lord, dear lord.'

CHAPTER 10

So, that's how it happened.

That's why, on this lovely Monday morning, we are sitting in Charlie's car as we head for the M40 in search of answers to the burning question: is Charlie's boyfriend a two-timing bastard, or a three-timing bastard, or entirely innocent of all charges?

'Where did you tell Ted you were going?' asks Juan as we listen to the sat nav telling us to come off the motorway.

'I lied. I knew he'd try and talk me out of it if I told him the truth. I said we were going to Wales to visit my friends Charlie and Eddie.'

'What if he contacts them?'

'Why in the name of the lord would he do that?'

'I don't know. Just think it might have been safer to be less specific.'

We drive along a windy road that goes underneath a pretty bridge before turning left into a very average-looking hotel. Let's be honest: it looks like a cheap B&B, or what do they call them in America? A motel. It looks like the sort of motel where people go for cheap sex or to get their heads down after a long day driving the truck.

'This can't be right,' says Juan. 'This is like something out of *Schitt's Creek*. Heavens alive, we must be able to do better than this.'

'I was stressed when I booked it. Give me a break,' says Charlie.

'OK, sorry, but this is not the place to base ourselves to conduct a major covert NYPD-style operation.'

'Let's just drop our things here, go for breakfast and make a plan,' says Charlie.

'Good. I'm bloody starving,' I reply.

I watch both Charlie and Juan smile. 'What's so funny?'

'Nothing. It's just that you're always starving.'

'Well, that's true.'

We carry our bags up to our rooms. We've got a bedroom each, which is rather extravagant of us, though I think I'd have preferred to share a room and be in a more salubrious hotel.

I open my luggage and pull out a ginger wig I plan to use if I need to disguise myself at any stage. I didn't bring a false beard, mainly because I don't have one, but also because Charlie and Juan insist that there will be no need to dress up. I do have a cowboy hat through which - I think we can all agree - will make for a fine disguise.

It takes less than 20 minutes to unpack the few things I've brought with me. I brush through my hair, slap on some lipstick and run back to reception, ready for a trip to the pub.

We end up at the Horse & Hounds - a rather lovely, terribly quaint pub with a huge menu of proper home-cooked pub grub.

'Right, what do you want to do? What's the fundamental

aim of this exercise,' says Juan, unfurling an A3-sized piece of paper and holding down the edges with these heavy, metal beer mats to keep it flat.

'I want to find the people sleeping with my boyfriend and kill them.'

'I was thinking of a less violent response, but let's go with that for now. The first thing we need to do is find the women. That shouldn't be too difficult...we've got contact details for both of them. The issue is: which one shall we contact first?'

'I think we should call Lola,' I say. 'It's much easier to call someone. We can hang up and say 'wrong number' if it all goes wrong. It's much harder to do that if we're on someone's doorstep.'

'Agreed?' says Juan, looking at Charlie. 'Does that plan sound OK to you, too?'

'Yep. Off you go, call her now. We might as well make the call while we're waiting for our food to come.' she replies.

She's looking straight at me.

'Me?' I say. 'You want me to ring her?'

'Yes, please.'

'Oh, right. What shall I say?'

I'll be honest; this has all taken an unfortunate turn. I assumed that Juan and I were there to support Charlie in her endeavours to track down and talk to the women. I didn't expect to be ringing Lola and asking her about her private life.

'I don't know,' says Charlie, starting to cry. 'This is all a ridiculous idea. What are we even doing here? What's the point of this? It's just pointless.'

'Look, don't worry. I'll call her and ask, gently, if she knows Mike and whether she is in a relationship with him.

If she says she is, I'll explain that he has just moved in with my friend and that she's being made a fool of.'

'Yep, that sounds gentle,' says Juan.

'Mate, you are welcome to make this call instead of me if you want.'

'No, you're good. This one's all yours.'

Juan changes my phone settings so that the person I'm calling can't see my number, and I dial the number on the back of the photo from the 'Confessions' box. A female voice answers straight away. She sounds very young. 'Hello, Oxford taxi driver,' she says.

'Is that Lola?' I ask.

'No, it's Jane. Can I help you?'

'I'd like to talk to Lola, please.'

'I'm sorry, she's not available at the moment. Did you want to book?'

Now it strikes me that booking a taxi driven by Lola will solve our problem perfectly. I will have time to talk to her. Indeed, I can sit there for as long as it takes to get her to open up, then Charlie can get into the taxi with us, and we can sort everything out. I give Charlie a big smile and a thumbs up.

'Yes, I'd like to book a taxi, please.'

'OK, let me take your name,' says Jane.

'Philomena Shiftalot,' I say.

I don't know why I said that. Really, I don't.

'That's an interesting name. Right. All booked. If you could come to 5 Castle Street at noon, we'll sort out the taxi driving.'

'See you then,' I say.

'She's a taxi driver,' I relay to Charlie and Juan triumphantly. 'And I've booked a ride in her taxi for noon so I can talk to her properly.'

'Great, is she picking you up from here?'

'No, she told me to go to Castle Street to get the cab.'

'Why? Surely the cab should come and pick you up from wherever you want it to.'

'Yes. I don't know. Perhaps it's for the security of the female drivers or something? It doesn't matter. I'll go there at noon, and we will find out everything.'

'Thanks, angel,' says Charlie, giving me a huge hug. 'You are the best person in the whole world.'

'That's true. I'm glad you all finally realise that.'

IT'S ONLY 11 AM, so after a very large English breakfast, we decide to use the free hour before my taxi ride to visit Anna. We have her address but no phone number, so we will have to do some door-knocking this time. I look up the address on my phone and discover it's walking distance from Castle Street.

'Anna and Lola are neighbours,' I say out loud. 'I wonder whether they know one another?'

'I still think they might be the same person,' says Juan, as we drive down quite a scruffy road until we get to a more salubrious area. The houses look bigger and more imposing...some of them have long driveways, and others have iron gates defending the perimeter of the properties.

'Here,' shouts Charlie. 'This is the address: Water Lodge.'

We pull up outside a large, red brick, Edwardian house. There's another one next door that is identical-looking. They are both very large homes, set back from the road, with lovely sash windows, and each with balconies.

'This is a proper grown-up's house,' I say. I note the immaculate garden, the garage and the beautiful wooden door with stained glass window panels. The fact that it's such a lovely, homely place is a little concerning. Can this be right? It looks like a place where a family or an older couple would live. It doesn't feel right for a young woman.

Charlie and I step out of the car without much of a clue about what comes next. Charlie looks at the big house and immediately gets back inside. She drops her head into her hands, and I see her shoulders shake slightly.

'Are you crying?' I ask.

'It's all so horrible,' she replies. 'Look at these amazing houses. Why is someone in a house like this sending love letters to my boyfriend? I don't understand at all.'

'I'm just about to find out. I will handle everything, don't worry.' I gently close the car door, and Juan and I walk around the driveway to the house, but I can't figure out which one is Anna's place. Halfway between the two houses, there's a sign saying 'Water Lodge.'

'We'll have to try both. Have you got your speech ready? Do you know what you're going to say?'

'No, of course, I don't. I'm just going to have to bullshit it. I might say I'm a saleswoman or something to get at talking and then say, 'do you know Mike?' I went to school with him and thought he might live here.'

Juan looks unimpressed by my suggested patter but doesn't offer an alternative scenario, so I decide to bulldoze through with my saleswoman line.

CHAPTER 11

I walk up to the door of the first extraordinarily lovely house and knock gently on the door. There's no reply.

I try again, but there's still no reply, and the house feels empty. Do you know what I mean? Sometimes you knock on a door and have a strong feeling that some- one's in there and feel minded to wait awhile to see whether they appear. This wasn't the case with this particular house.

'Let's try the other one,' I suggest to Juan, and walk back down the path, onto the pavement, and head towards the other house. But as I start along the path, a woman walks out.

'Is everything ok?' she asks.

'Which of the houses is Water Lodge?' I ask.

'Both,' she says. 'It's all one house.'

'Oh wow. I see. It's huge.'

'Indeed it is. I'm the housekeeper. Have you come to clean the pool?'

I'm wearing my new dress. Do I look like a bloody cleaner?

'I am looking for Anna Day, but she doesn't seem to be in.'

'No, she's at the hospital today,' says the woman.

'Oh, I'm sorry to hear that. Is everything OK?'

'Yes, Everything is proceeding as expected; nothing to worry about on that front. She's just gone to work.'

'OK,' I say.

'Whom shall I say called?' asks the woman.

'Philomena,' I reply. 'Tell her that Philomena Shiftalot was looking for her.'

'Oh,' says the housekeeper with a raised eyebrow. Perhaps they don't get too many Philomenas around here.

I walk back to the car to be greeted by two eager faces looking up at me like tiny birds waiting to be fed by their mother returning from a hunt.

'Don't get too excited...she wasn't there. I did talk to the housekeeper, though.'

'Housekeeper?' says Charlie.

'Oh yes. Those two houses aren't two houses at all but are one massive place. They have a pool. She thought I was the bloody pool cleaner.'

I await the exclamations of surprise that I could ever be confused with a pool cleaner, but nothing comes.

'Anyway, she says that Anna is in a hospital. When I asked if Anna was OK, she said something about everything proceeding as expected and that she was there to work, so I guess she's a nurse?'

'Or a doctor?' says Juan. 'Don't be so sexist.'

'Yep, she could be a brain surgeon. Good point, Juan.'

'Which hospital is she in?'

'I don't know. I said I was a friend, so I couldn't ask where she worked because a friend would know something like that. In any case, we can't go to the hospital, can we?'

'Of course, we bloody can,' says Charlie. 'That's exactly where we are going.'

'But I have my taxi ride.'

'We've got time to pop in quickly. It's almost an hour before you meet Lola.'

'Sure,' I say. I do seem to have the worst role in this research trio.

It turns out the nearest hospital is called Bradley Road. Once again, it's muggins here who is sent in to find out whether Anna is a staff member at the hospital, and if so - is she a brain surgeon or a cleaner?

I approach the reception desk and smile warmly at the woman sitting behind it. She has the distracted air of someone who mentally clocked out about two years ago.

'Yes...' she says.

'Oh, hello. I wondered whether Anna Day was available to come to reception. I'm a friend of hers, and she told me to pop in and ask for her at the main desk.'

'What department does she work in?'

'She works in this hospital.'

'Yes, I know. Do you know which department?'

'Sorry, I don't.'

The receptionist sighs deeply and taps away at a few keys before looking at me. 'Anna Day? We have an Anna Day in Accident and Emergency. Would that be her?'

'Yes, that's her,' I say. 'I'd like to speak to her, please.'

'She's working at the moment, and it's very busy. I don't think she'll be able to come out and see you. Why don't you text her and ask her when her shift ends and whether she can come and meet you then?'

'She doesn't have any breaks, does she? Maybe I could nip in and chat with her when she has a break.'

'She's a nurse in a busy A&E department; she's unlikely

to have a break. Maybe she worked in a post office, but not here.'

'Fine,' I say, and I spin on my heels, planning to storm away like a Hollywood star, but I sort of over-rotate on my heels and half fall before staggering away. It's not the exit I was hoping for.

I head back out to meet the others.

'She works in A&E. She won't be able to come to the reception desk because she is busy. The receptionist was very rude.'

'Yep, they always are. It's in the bible - if you work as a receptionist for a doctor or in a school, you have to be incredibly rude to everyone for no reason.'

'Her attitude has made me want to go and see Anna now. Shall we go to Accident & Emergency and see whether we can talk to her there?'

'Yes,' says Charlie with gusto. She doesn't seem at all tearful now. A quiet determination has replaced the misery.

We trundle off towards the A&E department, following the signs leading us all around the hospital's perimeter as we go. I am increasingly confident in asking for a woman I've never met for reasons I can't divulge. Amazing what you can become accustomed to.

But it's no good. Accident and Emergency are less helpful than the main desk. I'm told they can't give me information about when her shift ends and that my best bet is to contact her directly. In other words, 'GO AWAY.' At least we know where Anna works, though, and we know she's in there right now and will be out at some point today. It's not much to go on, but it's much more than we had earlier this morning.

I explain all this to Charlie and Juan, and the three of us find a bench to sit on while we assess our options.

'She's on an early shift if she's in the hospital at 11,' I rationalise. 'In which case, I guess she's probably working from 7 am until 3 pm or something? Do you think?'

'Christ, no idea,' says Charlie.

'No, me neither, I'm just guessing. Look - it's 11.30 am now, and I have to go to see Lola in half an hour, so why don't you two stay here, watch the hospital, and follow her when she comes out.'

'How can we? We don't have a clue what she looks like.'

'Oh God, No, we don't, do we? There were no pictures of her in the box. Let's try googling.'

'We tried that, remember. There was no picture.'

'Yes, but now we know her occupation, and where she works, we can narrow down all the options. She might even be on the hospital website.'

'Actually, that's a good shout,' says Charlie, pulling out her phone and beginning to input the information we have.

'Yes, there's a list of staff at the hospital...here we are... Oh no, it's just consultants.'

'Try Facebook,' offers Juan, pulling his phone out and joining the search.

It doesn't take long.

'Oh wow,' he says. 'She's on Linked In. 'Listen to this... Anna is a senior nurse at Bradley Road Hospital and has worked in A&E for the past two years. She undertook her training at Manley's Hospital in Bolton and has worked in Community and General Hospitals as well as General Practice.'

'Never mind all that,' says Charlie. 'I'm sure she's an absolute angel, but is there a photo of her?'

'Um...yeah.'

Juan holds up a picture of a woman who looks like a film star. The woman is stunning...glossy brown curls tumbling over her shoulders, big eyes, full lips, dimples...the whole nightmare.

'Let me see.' Charlie grabs the phone and enlarges it.

'Oh great,' she says.

'You don't know anything is happening between her and Mike.'

'It seems unlikely she'd be writing love letters to him if nothing was going on.'

'Well, yes, but - there could be a straightforward explanation.'

'Yeah, of course, there could. A gorgeous woman is sending my boyfriend love letters, but it could just be that they're friends.'

'At least we know what she looks like, so we should be able to spot her,' says Juan.

'I'm so thrilled that I know what she looks like,' says Charlie. 'I bet she gets dressed up in her nurse's uniform for him.'

'Stop it,' I say. 'We don't know anything; let's all calm down. There's no point in getting worried. I'm going to get a cab to see Lola, and you and Juan need to stay and stake out the hospital. Wait for Anna to appear, then follow her and try to talk to her. And remember to text me and tell me where you're going. I could even get Lola to drop me near you in the taxi.'

'Yes, OK,' says Charlie.

'I still think it's weird that you're getting a cab to go and get a cab,' says Juan as I walk away, calling an Uber on my phone.

'It doesn't matter. As long as I get to talk to Lola, it doesn't matter how I do it.'

'Just make sure you don't get kidnapped and sold into white slavery.'

'I'll do my best.'

I get out of the Uber and ring the doorbell. There's a long wait before a voice crackles over the intercom. 'It's Mary Brown.' I say. There's a click, the door opens, and I walk in, up a set of wooden stairs, and over to an Indian lady sitting at a trestle table at the top of the stairs. It's a really weird place, with stuffed animals on the walls wherever you look.

'Can I help you?' asks the lady.

'Sure,' I say, but I'm too busy looking at the array of woodland creatures stuffed and mounted onto the wall opposite to pay too much attention to her.

'Are you new to all this?' she says softly.

'To taxis?'

'Yes, have you done it before?'

'My God, of course. Yes - loads and loads of times.'

'Right, straight into the advanced group for you then. This is just a taster session, but you'll learn more about how it works.'

'Advanced group? Taster session? I don't understand.'

'Go through that door there and take a seat; Farah will be in to talk to you and explain how this will work.'

'I'm a bit confused.'

'Don't be; Farah will explain everything. Just head to that room, and have a sit-down. Oh, and as this is a trial, there's no charge.'

'Oh, that's good. Thank you.'

It's all weird, but at least it's free weirdness.

I walk into the small room, which smells strongly of bleach and vinegar. It's the oddest scent, like a cleaning solution, and strong vinegar have been sloshed all over the floors. The room is laid out like a craft room in a school, with glue, scissors, and various craft-making paraphernalia.

Two men are sitting there, both of whom look as if they've never seen daylight. I smile at them, sit down at the back, as far away from them as possible, and pull my phone out.

'I'm here, but I'm in a room that's like an arts and crafts room; not sure what's going on, but I will stick with it until I see Lola.' I text.

As I'm tucking my phone into my bag, a woman enters the room and walks to the front. She acknowledges the two men and looks over at me.

'Welcome,' she says. 'I see two familiar faces, but I don't know you. Would you like to tell me who you are?'

'My name is Mary Brown.'

'Well, welcome, Mary. It's lovely to see you. You are aware that this is an advanced class, aren't you? For those who are familiar with the art.'

'Yes,' I say.

'Good. Well, I hope you enjoy it. Do you all see the white carrier bag on the table in front of you?'

There is, indeed, a large white carrier bag in front of me.

'Put your hand in and pull out the contents,' she says.

As instructed, I put my hand into the bag and felt something with coarse hair inside. It's like a teddy bear, but the fur isn't soft and velvety. It feels unpleasant.

'Why are we doing this?' I ask.

'Bear with me, Mary. Just pull out the contents, and I'll explain.

'I'd rather not. Can't I get a taxi driven by Lola?'

'You want a taxi?'

'Yes, isn't that why we're here?'

She looks rather confused and urges me to remove the bag's contents.

I put my hand back into the bag and pull out a rather

bedraggled-looking fox. It feels real, but it obviously can't be. It's not like a toy fox, all fluffy and lovely - this is horrible.

'Just hold the fox in your hands and get used to the feeling of its fur while I'm talking to you.'

'Is it real?' I ask, standing up and jumping back, so my chair scrapes along the floor.

'Of course, it's real: what were you expecting?'

'I certainly wasn't expecting to be stroking a dead fox.' She looks at the other two members of the group, who seem to be perfectly at home with this bizarre, pre-taxi behaviour.

'Don't put the fox down until I say.'

'OK,' I reply.

I hold the fox, as instructed, but feel uncomfortable.

'That's it, just hold it and get used to how it feels.'

'How it feels is horrible,' I say.

'I understand. You've probably worked on mice and birds before. We're going to move on to foxes today. The tricks we'll teach you, and the artistry we will explore, will enable you to stuff pets and even stuff animals to exhibit them, so this is an exciting step forward in your taxidermy career.'

'Taxidermy?' I say.

'That's right, dear; this is a taxidermy course.'

'No, there's been a mistake. I wanted to book a taxi.'

'A taxi? What do you mean, a taxi? We can organise a taxi for you at the end if you need one. Or there is a very good bus service here.'

'No, you don't understand. This is all a horrible mistake. I want to talk to Lola, and I want to talk to her in the taxi.'

'Lola?'

'Yes, she's a taxi driver, no?'

'No, she is a junior taxidermist here; she's just started teaching. This is the Oxfordshire Taxidermy Academy.'

'Well, I don't want to do taxidermy.'

'Well, you might be in the wrong place then.'

'Is Lola here today? I just wanted to see her, so I booked a taxi with her…to talk to her.'

'No, Lola is not here. She works during the day. She comes here in the evenings, one day a week, to help and get teaching experience.'

'Oh right.'

'So, are you staying with us?'

' Heavens, no,' I say, standing up and backing out of the room, apologising and wishing them happy taxidermy. I retreat into the hallway, where the stuffed animals lining it suddenly make much more sense.

'Everything okay?' asks the lady on the makeshift reception desk.

'Yes, I'm not going to do the course, thank you very much. All a bit confusing, really. Good luck with everything.'

I run down the stairs to the front door at the bottom and swing it open, calling for an Uber as I go. I stand on the street outside, waiting for my car to arrive and whisk me away from this place when my phone pings to indicate a message.

'We're on the move…come when you can, we are following Anna.'

CHAPTER 12

I push the doors to the pub and spot Juan and Charlie loitering by the bar with three glasses of wine in front of them. Perfect.

'What the hell is that?' asks Juan, staring open-mouthed at me.

'What is what?' I ask. He appears to be pointing at my stomach. Has he only just realised that I'm fat?

'That!'

He steps in to point directly at the dead fox that I am still carrying under my arm.

'Oh, that! Yes, that's a long story.'

'I don't care how long the story is. I need to know how you couldn't talk to Lola and have returned clutching a dead fox.'

'She's not a taxi driver; she's a taxidermist. I was booked onto a taxidermy course.'

'Oh my God, that's the funniest thing I've ever heard,' says Juan. 'A taxidermy course?'

'Yes. And the ridiculous thing is that I would have done the bloody course if she'd been running it to be able to chat with her, but she works during the day and goes there at night as a student teacher. There were dead, stuffed animals everywhere.'

Under normal circumstances, this would be the signal for much hilarity from Charlie. But so spectacularly ridiculous is my story that she stands there and stares at me.

'Taxidermy?' she says, eventually.

'Yes. They were teaching us how to stuff animals. It was a taster course.'

'So you haven't spoken to Lola?'

'No, I haven't been near Lola; I've been learning the basics of taxidermy. I'm going to keep hold of this fox so we can go back there and return it when Lola's around so we can talk to her. Where's Anna?'

'She's in that group there, with those other women,' says Juan. 'There - at the far end of the bar.'

I can't pick Anna out from the cluster of young women around her. There must be around 30 of them.

'Are you going to go and talk to her?' asks Juan. He and Charlie are both looking at me.

'Me? Why is this all coming down to me?'

'I don't want to go and talk to her,' says Charlie.

'OK, OK. I'm going to have this glass of wine first. I must recover from the drama of spending time locked in a room with dead things.'

'Charlie looks at me, her eyes slowly filling with tears.'

'OK, let's go,' I say, taking a big gulp of wine. The two of us push our way along the bar so we can loiter close to the group.

'Can you see her?' says Charlie. I look over but can't work out which one Anna is. I suspect that Charlie has studied the photo of her love rival more closely than I have.

'She's in that black dress with gold buttons. The dress

that's too short and trying too hard to look like Chanel when it's clearly from some High Street shop.'

This is uncharacteristically bitchy of Charlie. She never talks about people like that.

I look over again and see Anna throwing her head back as she laughs at a joke. The really bad news for my lovely friend is that Anna is spectacularly attractive. She's got the hair that everybody wants, I mean *everyone*. Big bouncy curls, glossy with health and rippling over her shoulders. I'm too far away to study her closely, but she is slim and elegant-looking, and her face is exceptionally pretty.

'She's not all that,' I say.

'I was worried that everyone would think she's really attractive. She's not, though, is she?'

'No. Not at all. Quite average-looking.'

'And her dress is way too short.'

It's not. The dress is lovely, and the woman has great legs.

'Way too short.' I say.

We edge over until we are standing right next to the group.

'OK, everyone,' says a large man at the bar. He has a faintly American accent. 'Let's down these drinks, and on we go.'

With that, the assembled group knock back their drinks and begin shuffling around, chatting and collecting bags before heading towards the door.

Charlie glances at me, and I signal Juan to come over and join us.

'It looks like they're going.'

'Have you spoken to her yet?' he asks.

'I haven't had the chance. I was hoping she would go to the loo and I could follow her, or the group would disperse a little bit so I could get close to her. But now it looks like they're all leaving.'

'We'll have to go after them, but we need to get alongside her,' he says. 'We can't just stalk her.'

'Yes, we all know that,' says Charlie.

CHAPTER 13

Staying at a sensible distance, we follow behind the group of young nurses - mainly women, with half a dozen men in their midsts. They are chatting as they go, linking arms, and having a rather lovely time of it. It must be nice to work with people you like. There are a few people at work who I get on with, but would I want to go out and socialise with them? In a pub? Arm-in-arm? Nah!

We approach a pub called The Barley Mow, and the group disappear inside.

'I think we might be stalking a nurses' pub crawl,' says Juan. 'If I weren't gay, this would be my dream come true.'

'We can't stalk a pub crawl,' says Charlie. 'This is all quite ridiculous now.'

'No, it's all fine,' I insist. 'We'll grab her for five minutes in this pub; then we'll leave. We've tried so hard to find her; we can't give up now. And I really don't want to go back to that taxidermy school.'

Charlie walks through the crowd to get to the bar, hoping to bump into Anna, who seems to have disappeared. 'Follow me,' she shouts as she launches herself into a small gathering near the bar in search of our target. I trundle along behind and see Anna up ahead.

Charlie has stopped about a metre in front of her and is just standing, staring. It's like she's transfixed.

'Is everything OK?' asks Anna.

I bolt past Charlie and straight up to Anna. 'Everything is absolutely fine. I'm Mary, by the way. And this is my best friend, Charlie.'

Anna and I shake hands.

'What's that?' says Anna, pointing at the dead fox.

'Oh, just something for a friend.'

'Have you been doing taxidermy?'

'Yes, I have. How do you know about taxidermy?'

'I know someone who does it. I think it's a very odd thing to do. Look, is your friend OK?'

Charlie stands still and stares at Anna as if she's never seen anything like it.

'You're very pretty,' she says, eventually.

Anna's not sure what to say, so she half-smiles and turns back to the group next to her. I can't let her get back into a conversation with them.

'We were at the hospital earlier. I think I recognise you. But we haven't met properly.'

'Oh, I see. Sorry, I didn't recognise you. Are you with the visiting team?'

'Yes,' I say, almost punching the air with relief. A visiting ream. The perfect cover.

'Lovely to meet you. Brilliant. You guys are phenomenal. Hey, Kat. This is Mary and Charlie; they are with the team of visiting professors.'

'Oh, how impressive. Lovely to meet you,' says Kat, giving me a huge hug before moving in to embrace Charlie, stopping short of touching her, sensing the animosity surrounding her like a shield.

'Good, right. OK. Which group are you with? Paediatric pulmonology or urologic oncology?'

'Yes, that's right,' I say with enthusiasm.

'No, which one?' Anna laughs as she says this, and I feel I might be slightly out of my depth.

'The first one.'

'Pediatric pulmonology?'

'Yes.'

'That's an interesting area of medicine,' she says. 'What made you decide to pursue it?'

'It just really interests us, doesn't it, Charlie?'

'Yes, it's very interesting.'

'I didn't see you at the presentation earlier. I'm sure we'd remember you if you'd been there. You don't exactly look like the others,' says Kat.

'No, we weren't there. Not all of us were at the presentation.'

'Oh, I see. I thought they said you'd all come on the same flight.'

'Yes, but we had to do some other things first.'

'I see. Are you from the UK originally? Or have you always lived in Nigeria?'

Charlie deserts me at this point. I guess the realisation that she's pretending to be a visiting professor from Nigeria, specialising in an area of medicine we have no understanding of, is a little too much for her.

It might be too much for me too.

'Excuse me,' I say, backing away. 'It's lovely to see you, but I have to call the hospital in Nigeria.'

When I arrive at the table commandeered by Juan, I find Charlie sobbing her heart out.

'She's so beautiful, so beautiful,' she's saying.

Juan is making things infinitely worse with his efforts to help her.

'I bet they aren't having an affair. If she's that beautiful, then there's no way she can be by having a fling with Mike, is there?'

'What are you saying?' asks Charlie.

'No, I'm not saying that an attractive person wouldn't be with Mike. I'd say that it's unlikely.'

'Not making this any better,' says Charlie.

'No, I mean - she's supposed to be having an affair with him. Why would she be? Why would she need to go out with someone else's boyfriend if she's very attractive and could easily find a man of her own? That's all I'm saying.'

'Mary told them we were visiting doctors with weird specialisms,' Charlie responds.

'I didn't realise they were visiting from Nigeria,' I confess. 'We probably don't look very Nigerian, do we? Her friend just knew we were making it all up.'

'Well, yeah. You're the wrong age, wrong colour, the wrong sex, and you're carrying a dead fox around.'

'But, besides that, we look the part...'

'Did you ask her *anything* about her boyfriend?' says Juan. 'No,' I confess. 'It's just too hard there, with all those people around. I started chatting to her and planned to go into the whole subject, but got distracted by the visiting professors thing.'

The three of us look back at the large group of medics, now looking as if they are preparing to move on.

'Shall we follow them?' I ask.

'No,' says Charlie. 'Let's go back to her house in the morning and talk to her one-to-one.'

CHAPTER 14

Bright-eyed and bushy-tailed, we're back at Anna's house the next morning, sitting in the car down the side road next to her massive mansion. This woman's husband must be incredibly rich. There's no way a nurse would earn enough to afford this place. Christ, there's no way I'd risk my marriage for a fling with Mike.

'She won't be here. She'll be at work,' says Charlie. The woman has lost all faith in this undercover investigation. It's hard to see why. I mean - everything's going so well.

'If she is, we'll just come back later...we talked about this,' I say.

We discussed whether we should come over this early. Since she was on the early shift yesterday, it was likely that she would be again today. We would just come back later if she wasn't here.

I approach the door, where there's a cleaner polishing the front doorstep.

'Can I help you?' she asks.

I don't know quite what to say, and I'll admit that I feel a little hung over. We stayed in the pub drinking for hours after Anna and her colleagues left, then moved to the terrible bar at the B&B, where I kept holding up my dead fox and introducing him to people.

'I'm looking for Anna,' I say.

'She's at work,' she responds. 'Why do you want her?'

'I'm selling things. She is interested in what I'm selling, so

I said I'd come along to show her my wares.' 'What are you selling?'

'Pegs.'

'Pegs?'

'Yep.'

'Can I see them?' she asks.

'No,' I reply. 'Not unless you want to buy them. I'll come back later and talk to her.'

This is becoming ridiculous. I'm not knocking on her door anymore.

At 2 pm, we head back to the hospital. I have to say that this is all feeling a little déjà vu.

'If I go in there, they won't let me see her,' I say. 'We need to think of a clever plan.'

'I know,' says Juan. 'I should ring up and say there's a messenger outside. I'll say the message is very important, and could she come out and get it.'

'They'll send security out,' replies Charlie. 'That won't work.'

'No, I've got it,' says Juan, wide-eyed. He's clearly had a first-rate idea, and I'm dreading hearing what it is.

'You go in there and pretend you've got an injury and ask to see a nurse. Our target works in A&E. She'll be the one who sees you. This is perfect.'

'Yes!!' shouts Charlie. 'Perfect!'

'Um...not exactly perfect, though, is it? I'll have to gain

entry to the hospital by deception, then try to talk to a nurse who is bound to be dealing with another patient.'

But Charlie is hooked. She is squealing 'yes' a lot.

'I mean - why didn't we do this before?' she says.

'We didn't think of it before because it's got disaster written all over it, and anyone mad enough to go into a busy accident and emergency hospital and take up doctors' and nurses' valuable time with a fake injury should be shot.'

'No, you won't take up anyone's time because you'll tell her straight away that you're really sorry you don't have an injury, but there's something you need to ask her, then you tell her that you think she's going out with Charlie's boyfriend, and judge her reaction.'

I know this is going to go wrong, but the other two aren't listening.

I decide to give it one last try: 'Wouldn't it be a million times better if Charlie were the one to confront her? I mean, how can it work if it's me doing it?'

'I can't, I can't,' Charlie says, dropping her head into her hands. 'I only want to know. Can't you go in and ask her? It can't be that hard, can it?'

'Okay,' I say. 'I'll do it.' Honestly, I'm such a soft touch.

CHAPTER 15

I adopt a hunched position and shuffle towards the hospital to tell the waiting nurses about my injured neck. I'm getting into the part by the time I get close to the front doors of the Accident & Emergency department. My grimace is good, and the hunch is coming along nicely. People are looking at me sympathetically. I'm giving off the full 'hunchback of Notre Dame' vibe.

But then I have a panic...what if they diagnose some terrible neurological condition, and I'm lined up for a brain operation. No, I don't want that. I need a much lower-key injury. With great dexterity, I swing from hunching to limping. I've injured my ankle. I stagger towards the A&E department reception desk with a pained look and a significant stagger to my legs.

I tell the receptionist about my tumble down the curb. I explain how I landed in the gutter in agony and managed to clamber back onto my feet, but I think I may have broken my ankle.

'Is it swollen?' she asks without looking up at me. 'Yes, very swollen and very sore.'

'Have you ever injured it before?'

Now there's a question I hadn't anticipated.

'Yes, once before,' I say, for no good reason.

'How did you hurt it then? Did you break it?'

Why didn't I say I'd never injured it before?

'I was playing football for the ladies' first team, and I fell when scoring a goal. Twisted it. Nasty.'

She looks up fleetingly, presumably taking in my size and wondering how fat the second team players must be, then dutifully writes down the story I'm telling her before asking me to take a seat in the waiting room.

My God, if I don't get offered a role in *Casualty* after this, there's no justice in the world.

I know that the waiting room is my route to Anna. I can't go further with the deception because any nurse worth her salt will look at my entirely uninjured ankle and say, 'it's uninjured.' But at least I'm now in the heart of the A&E department, and as soon as I see Anna, I'll jump up and drag her to one side and beg her to answer my questions.

The waiting room is quite busy, so I settle into one of the uncomfortable plastic seats and pull out my mobile phone to send a text.

'BREAKING NEWS: I'm in the waiting room. No sign of Anna yet. Will let you know as soon as there's a sighting.'

I look up and smile at the guy next to me. He's painfully skinny and rather unclean-looking in a khaki jacket and tracksuit bottoms.

'What have you done?' he asks.

I tell him the story about how I was playing football when I went over on it. 'I was just about to score when I crashed to the ground.'

When I'm halfway through the story, I remember this anecdote about how I injured it the first time.

'How about you?'

He lifts his arm up, and his finger is going off in the wrong direction. It's broken or dislocated or something.

'I was pissed,' he explains.

A middle-aged woman who looks much like Clare Balding is on my right. She appears to have her entire family with her.

'Sorry, but I couldn't help overhearing. Did you say you injured your ankle playing ladies' football?'

'That's right,' I say.

A young woman, who I assume is her daughter, comes over and sits on the floor in front of me.

'Who do you play for?' she asks.

'England,' I reply.

'Wow!' 'Gosh!' 'My goodness!'

The thrill of being in the presence of an England football international is palpable. I only said 'England' because I don't know the names of any women's football teams. To say I regret saying that now would be an understatement.

'Tell us what it's like to run out for your country,' says the young woman on the floor. She looks starstruck, and I regret having started this stupid conversation.

'It makes you feel very proud, very alive. It's magnificent,' I say.

There are gasps from my small audience and a gentle ripple of applause.

'Thank you,' I say bashfully before continuing to extoll the joys of playing international football.

'Marjorie Watkins,' shouts a nurse. 'Is there a Majorie Watkins?'

I look up to see Anna.

'That's me,' I say, standing up.

'Be careful,' says the man with the wonky finger. 'Mind your ankle.'

I hobble over to Anna while the Clare Balding look-alike holds one arm and her daughter holds the other, helping me while I stumble and grimace.

'Look after her,' she says to Anna. 'She's a sporting superstar.'

I hobble after Anna, overdoing the limp to such an extent that I look like I have a wooden leg. I hear a lady behind me shouting, 'Excuse me, excuse me,' and can only assume that's the real Marjorie wondering why I have nicked her appointment.

We go into one of those cubicles with curtains around the edge of it, and she looks from the file in her hand to me with confusion across her incredibly pretty face.

'Okay, a couple of things... this file says you are 64 and are having palpitations brought on by the cancer medication you're taking. That doesn't sound like you. And what sporting superstar are you? I'm very confused. Also - I'm sure I recognise you from somewhere?'

'I've done a terrible thing. I've lied to you in order to talk to you. I'm a bad person.'

'And don't I know you from somewhere,' she says. 'Aren't you a visiting professor? Did we meet last night?'

'No, no, you must be thinking of someone else,' I say. 'But please let me just ask you something.'

'Yes, we did; I remember now – you had a dead fox with you. Why are you running around with dead foxes, pretending to be Marjorie, and claiming to be part of the visiting professorship from Nigeria? I'm calling security.'

'OK, look, I understand that this doesn't look good. But there is a straightforward explanation,' I say.

'I can't wait to hear it.'

Before she can call security, I burst into the story. I tell her that my lovely friend Charlie has just moved in with her boyfriend Mike and found letters from her, and I suspect she might be seeing Mike as well.

She stares at me.

'Do you have a boyfriend called Mike?'

'No, I don't have a boyfriend. I'm married with a child, and I'm six months pregnant. My husband is called Michael, but he never goes by 'Mike', and he certainly doesn't have a girlfriend, so you can tell your friend she's on the wrong track, and if you ever darken the doors of this hospital again with your lies, I will call security straight away.'

'I completely understand; you are absolutely right. I'm going to go now,' I say.

I stand up, push back the curtain and run out of the cubicle and into the waiting area.

'Oh my God! You're better.' shouts the Clare Balding look alike, staring at my suddenly healed ankle.

'I know. It's a miracle!' I shout back. 'That nurse is a miracle worker.'

There are cheers around the waiting room and genuine joy that my international career is back on track.

As I run out of the hospital, I see a grey-haired woman at reception complaining that a fat lady stole her appointment.'

'I'm sure that's not the case,' I hear the receptionist reply. 'You just need to wait until you're called.'

'But I was called, and a woman pretended to be me...'

CHAPTER 16

'Did you talk to her?' asks Charlie.

'Yes, I spoke to her. She's not seeing Mike. She's married and expecting her husband's baby.'

'She's married? Really?'

'Not only married but pregnant. She was quite cross when I accused her of having an affair with my friend's boyfriend.'

'I bet she was,' says Juan. 'What did you do when she said that?'

'I apologised for wasting her time and jumped up and ran out.'

'On your broken ankle?'

'Yep, on my broken ankle. All the waiting room cheered when they saw my miraculous recovery....they were thrilled that I could now resume my international football career.'

'Your what?'

'Long story.'

'That's so weird. I can't make any sense out of that,' Charlie is muttering to herself. 'If she's married and expecting her husband's child, then she isn't going out with

Mike. So the question now is why on earth are there letters, which seemed to be from her, in Mike's confession box? They must be having an affair. Could they, do you think?'

'No, honestly, mate. The look on her face...she looked disgusted. There is no way that she's the woman seeing Mike.'

'But the letters...'

'I know. But it's not her.'

'Is there another Anna, do you think?'

I suppose there must be, but the letters were sent from her address, and we went to that address.'

'Yes, but we didn't see Anna at that address.'

'Oh blimey, I bet that's what's happened. We've got the wrong, Anna, haven't we? There must be two Annas working at the hospital. It's the only explanation.'

While we attempt to analyse the bizarre situation we find ourselves in, my phone rings. It's a number I'm not familiar with, so I immediately think it must be Anna calling me. Or maybe Anna's husband, wondering why I'm accusing his wife of having an affair. Or possibly Marjorie, whose appointment I stole, the visiting professors from Nigeria, or the taxidermy school asking for their fox back...Let's be honest; it could be any number of people.

I answer the phone cautiously to hear a male voice with a slight accent that I don't immediately understand.

'It's Charlie here,' he says.

'Errr...Charlie is standing right next to me,' I say. 'Who is this?'

'It's Charlie Gower. Do you remember me?'

'Oh my God! Charlie Gower. Sorry, I'm away from home, investigating, and I got all caught up in the details. Of course, I remember you. Of course. How are you? How's Eddie? How's life on the farm?'

'Everything Is absolutely fine. The farm's going brilliantly, and Eddie and I are both well. I'm just calling you because I had an odd message on WhatsApp about 20 minutes ago and thought I'd better tell you.'

'Really? How can I help?'

'Well, it was from Ted, your boyfriend. He said that you were in Wales visiting me and he wanted to come out for a surprise visit. He asked whether it would be OK to turn up at 3 pm this afternoon, stay for the evening, and then head back tonight. He asked me not to tell you he was coming, so it's a surprise. But I didn't even know you were coming to visit. I'm completely confused.'

'Oh no, this is embarrassing. I told Ted I was going to Wales to visit you, but I went to Oxford to check whether this guy was two-timing my friend. But we got the wrong nurse. I think. I don't know. Charlie, it's very complicated.'

'Yes, it sounds like it. What would you like me to reply to Ted?'

'Is it OK if two friends and I come to visit you today?'

'Of course.'

'And could you tell Ted that we came yesterday?'

'If you want me to.'

'Good. We're leaving now.'

I put down the phone and look over at the confused faces of Charlie and Juan.

'Guys, I know this is a bit weird, but we'll need to go to Wales to see Charlie and Eddie. Ted's on his way there to pay me a surprise visit.'

'But what about Anna?' cries Charlie.

'Yes, I know. I promise that we'll come back here as soon as we've done the Wales bit.

'You're joking. Mary, we can't just go off to Wales. It's miles.'

'I know, but I'll get in trouble if we don't.'

'Is there no way you could just ring Ted and tell him that you're not in Wales after all?'

'I'd rather not. Let's go for one night; then we can return, feeling fresh, and continue the search.'

We leave most of our stuff behind in the B&B and bring only the bare essentials. Of course, I bring my ginger wig in case a sudden need to be undercover arises. Charlie and Juan have only their hand luggage. We throw it all into the boot and head west. There's a great silence in the car as we drive along. I know they are both pissed off with me for insisting on this ridiculous diversion, but I don't want Ted to get suspicious or worried about what I've been up to when we've just moved in together.

We come off the motorway and begin the journey through the windy country lanes until we reach the narrow farmers' lanes that I remember from my previous trips to Wales.

We're making pretty good time as we race along, hoping to get there before Ted, but we are running dangerously low on petrol. When we see a garage, we know we have to stop.

'Can you get me some crisps and a Twix while you're in there?' I ask Charlie, handing her £30 for petrol and snacks.

While she's filling up, a woman comes to the car and stares at us. She's in her late 60s, at a guess, and has what looks like a terrible home perm. She's wearing an anorak zipped all the way up and is clearly distressed about something. She keeps walking around the car, stopping and staring before writing something down.

'Is she writing down our registration?' I say to Juan.

'I don't know; this is odd. She's just staring at the car.

Eventually, she walks away and my phone rings. It's

Charlie and Eddie; they've just had a call from Ted, who is about 10 minutes away.

'Oh blimey, we are about 10 minutes away as well,' I say, waving my arms at Charlie, who is emerging from the garage clutching confectionery.

'Ted's almost there,' I shout to her. 'You better get your foot down; if we're not there before him, he's going to wonder what is going on.'

Charlie jumps back into the car, throws crisps and chocolate at me, and drives tentatively down the long narrow country lanes. 'I can't see around any bends; there is no way I can go fast,' she says.

'I know, but Ted is hot on our tails; we must get there before him.'

'OK, but you're paying for the damage if I have a crash.'

With that, Charlie puts her foot down, and we move at some speed down the narrow country lanes. God only knows what will happen if we come across a car coming towards us. Happily, there are no on-coming vehicles, and Gower Farm soon hoves into view. We see Charlie and Edward standing outside, ready to greet us.

'Come in, come in,' they shout. 'He's not here yet.'

We lock the car and all dash into the farmhouse, kicking off our shoes and throwing ourselves onto the sofas just before Ted turns up.

We make it with minutes to spare. There is a gentle rap on the door, then some whispering in the hallway as he sneaks in on his surprise visit. I hear, 'don't tell her it's me', then he bursts in.

'Surprise!' he shrieks, and we're all forced to adopt a look of utter shock and amazement.

'What are you doing here?'

'You know, I was on the M4, heading to a meeting, and it

was cancelled; I was about to turn around and go home, then I thought - no, I'll go and surprise Mary in Wales.'

'How lovely,' I reply.

'Just divine. Always great to surprise people,' adds Juan with so little sincerity that I think he will give the whole game away.

'You OK, Charlie? You're very quiet,' he says as Charlie stares at her phone.

'Yes, just googling something. Very good surprise, Ted. Top-notch.'

'Right, well, are you going to show me round this lovely farm then, Mary? Show me where everything is?'

'Yes, of course,' I say, glancing at Eddie for help.

'Let's go in here first.'

I open a large wooden door into what I imagine will be the kitchen. It leads into a store cupboard. 'That's where they keep things,' I say. 'You always need places to keep things on a farm.'

CHAPTER 17

Eddie steps ahead of me and swings open the kitchen door. 'This door's a bit stiff,' he says. 'Let me open it for you.'

I raise my eyebrows to say 'thank you' as Ted steps into the kitchen and admires the huge, ancient Aga sitting resplendent on the far side of the room.

'Wow, have you used this since you've been here, Mary?' he asks.

'Sort of,' I reply.

'Well, it all looks very nice.'

'Do you fancy a cup of tea, Ted? We can give you the tour later. I'm sure you'd like to sit down and chat with Mary.'

'Actually, I might use your loo, if that's OK?' he says.

'Long journey and all that.'

I enter the main sitting room to find Charlie staring at her phone.

'I don't know what to make of all this,' she says. 'I don't understand any of it. Mike has sent me all these lovey-dovey texts, and he keeps telling me how much he loves me and wants to be with me forever. We've only just moved in together. We love each other. Nothing makes any sense.'

'Perhaps he's not having an affair. There might be a simple explanation,' says Juan, but I can tell that even he doesn't believe that.

'What simple explanation? OK, so it might not be the Anna that we have been stalking, but we know there's Anna involved here somewhere. I've got the letters, for God's sake. Something's going on.'

'Don't worry, angel. We'll head straight back to Oxford in the morning, and we won't leave until we have all the answers,' I say confidently.

'Oh damn,' says Juan. 'Damn, damn, damn.'

'What?'

'My new lodger has turned up at the flat. I forgot that I told him to come today.'

'Who? Andrew?'

'Yes. I said I'd meet him at the flat three hours ago. I had my phone in my bag. He's been calling and texting for hours. Shit.'

'Call him now,' I say. 'If you apologise profusely and ask him to hang on for another couple of days, you'll be back.'

Juan attempts to ring Andrew as Ted returns from his toilet visit and his brief wander around the farmhouse.

'Lovely place, isn't it?' he says.

'Oh, it's great,' I agree.

'The view from your window is amazing. Have you ever seen anything like it before?'

'Never,' I reply because it feels like the sort of response that he is after.

'Very tidy you all are, too; the rooms don't look like anyone is staying in them.'

'Yes,' I say. Nodding warmly.

'Well, that's completely screwed,' says Juan, dramatically pushing his phone into his pocket.

'He's been sitting outside the house for over three hours with all his stuff, and he's really upset. He doesn't want to move in with someone who can't remember that he's due to arrive, so he's going back to live with his parents.

'Oh no. But he was the only decent person we spoke to. Can't you make him change his mind?'

'I tried, but he's not listening to me. He wants me to refund his deposit.'

'That is a ginormous pain in the bum.'

Juan is shaking his head at the situation, Charlie is shaking her head at the situation, and I'm smiling inanely at Ted as he asks me what I've been doing while we've been here.

'We've been helping with the animals,' I say.

'Lovely.'

'Talking about the animals - it's milking time. Are you coming?' says Eddie. 'You can all learn what real farming is about.'

Ted jumps up. 'Wouldn't miss it for the world,' he says. 'I've always thought I'd make a pretty decent farmer.'

I follow him outside and trail behind as he, Charlie and Edward lead the way to the cows.

Juan and female Charlie stay inside, both looking as if they've just heard that the world is about to explode.

'This is the milking shed,' says Charlie as we walk past a big, ugly building with a corrugated iron roof. 'We've got Llyr working with us today; he'll be getting everything ready while we go up and get the cows.'

I march behind them in my ballerina flats, thinking that Ted must think me nuts to have left for a trip to a farm with no Wellington boots. Happily, Ted is so entranced by the sheep dogs running around our feet and the prospect of them rounding up cows and bringing them into the milking shed that the last thing on his mind is my footwear.

'What happens if you can't get the cows to come?' he asks.

'We have to get them to come. They have to be milked,' says Eddie as he opens the rusty gate, and we step into the muddy field. I feel my feet sink with every step. My pink ballerina flats and my feet and ankles are now brown. Eddie shouts instructions in Welsh to the dogs, and they head off at huge speed, going round and round the edge of the cows who have gathered in the centre of the field.

The dogs' circles become smaller, so they run closer to the cows, and then they start running in arcs behind the group of cows, forcing the animals forwards and towards the fence. Charlie and Eddie split up, with Eddie waiting near the gate while Charlie moves to the back of the herd of cows and shouts in Welsh. Whatever he says forces the dogs to run faster and makes the cows move faster through the gate, where Eddie leads them down the track towards the milking parlour. He's carrying a stick which he holds out in front of him as he goes. It's all quite thrilling to watch.

I'm now up to my calves in mud, and when I lift my legs, I'm not sure my shoes will stay on my feet.

The cows trot along with their huge pendulous udders swinging as they go. Like me, when I attempt to run without a bra on. Maybe I don't have a weight problem: maybe I need to be milked.

I don't share this observation with our farmers, of course. All three of them are now in the milking shed - two putting the suckers onto the giant teats of the cows the other herding them in and out to a waiting pen. The process takes a couple of hours before we walk them back up to the field.

'See you in the morning,' says Eddie, waving at the cows as Llyr closes the gate and walks away from the field. Charlie ruffles Eddie's hair affectionately as they go, and I'm suddenly overcome with emotion. I wish I had a kid brother or sister. How lovely that must be.

Ted and I walk back to the farmhouse while the farmers clean up the milking shed and ensure that the milk is all in the huge vat at the front of the farm, ready for the tanker.

I walk up to the farmhouse and see Juan outside, on the low stone wall, looking all worried.

'Hey, stop worrying,' I say to him, ruffling his hair in the same friendly way I watched Charlie do to Eddie.

'Stop!' he squeals. 'You're messing up my style. What are you doing? Never touch my hair. Do you hear - never touch my hair again.'

'Sorry,' I say. 'Just trying to be friendly.'

I sit myself down next to him, and Ted sits next to me. Before long, Charlie comes out of the farmhouse with cups of tea for us all.

We're all sipping our tea and enjoying the sight of fields and trees as far as the eye can see when a car comes along the narrow road to the farm.

'It's a police car,' says Ted as it gets closer.

We all sit up straight, immediately casting our minds back to work out what we might have done wrong. I've done quite a lot wrong in the past 24 hours.

'How can we help you?' I ask nervously, feeling sure that this visit is something to do with me.

'Do you live here?'

'No, we're just visiting. Charlie and Eddie are out finishing the milking.'

'Is this your car?' asks the officer.

'It's mine,' says Charlie.

'Do you have the keys,' says the officer.

'Yes, of course.'

'Could you get them for me?'

'Why? I don't understand. What's the problem?'

'We believe there is a body in the boot,' says the officer.

'What? That's ridiculous,' says Charlie.

'If you get the keys, we can sort this out straight away. If not, we'll have to take you to the station.'

Charlie jumps up and walks inside, glancing at me as she goes.

A few minutes later, she emerges, clutching the keys. 'Come with us, please,' they say, taking the keys and leading her towards the car.

They look at the boot and shout 'step back' to her. Charlie takes a huge step back as the officer cautiously opens the boot, and we all realise immediately what the problem is.

My ginger wig has caught in the boot door.

'Oh Christ,' says the officer, lifting out the piece of shiny, ginger hair. 'Thank God for that. I've not been on a murder investigation before.'

'I thought we were on for a minute there,' laughs the other officer. 'When I saw those strands of hair hanging through the boot door. Bloody hell.'

As the men heave sighs of relief, and I taketh wig from them, we see Charlie and Eddie walking towards the farmhouse.

'What's going on here?' says Eddie. 'Are you arresting us?'

'No, you're OK for now. We had a call-in. A woman saw this car at Pentallorgon garage and thought they had a body in the boot. We've just checked, and it's the lady's wig poking out of it.'

'A wig?' says Eddie. 'Why would you have a wig on the farm?'

'Same reason she's wearing flip-flops in the mud, I suppose,' says the Police Officer.

Everyone's eyes turn to look at my feet.

'They're ballet flats,' I shout. 'Ballet flats. Perfectly accept- able summer footwear.'

CHAPTER 18

'This is now becoming farcical,' says Charlie as we climb back into her car the next morning.

'It's not that farcical. We'll go back now and sort it all out.'

'Not farcical? Are you kidding? In the past two days, you've done taxidermy, had a fake ankle injury, a fake international football career, you've been a fake peg saleswoman, a friend called Philomena and a fake visiting professor from Nigeria. We've had to travel to another country to escape your boyfriend, and we've milked cows and fed chickens.'

'And she almost got arrested for murder,' adds Juan, rather unhelpfully.

'Yeah, well, I suppose when you put it like that, it's not been ideal, but we'll find out what's going on once and for all now - you'll see. Nothing else can go wrong.'

There's silence in the car.

The drive back to Oxford is nowhere near as stressful as the drive to Wales, battling against the traffic to be there before Ted. We're soon at the terrible B&B and sitting in the small restaurant, considering what to do next.

'What else can we do but go back to Anna's house and explain everything?'

'It's 4 pm; she could actually be there this time.'

'Yeah, but she's not going to let you in; she thinks you've lost your mind.'

'You and Charlie will have to go and talk to her then,' I say. 'I'm very happy to stay out of any further interactions with anyone on this trip. I seem to get everything wrong and attract loads of trouble.'

'No, you don't; you've been amazing,' says Charlie. 'Honestly, Mary. I don't know what I'd do without you. You're the best friend in the world.'

We decide to head back to Anna's, and this time we will all approach her, but there's no answer at the mansion, so we sit in the car to wait. Then we see a woman walking towards the house. It's not Anna from yesterday, but a much slighter, mousey-looking woman. Young, with straight hair. It must be another cleaner. This place is better-staffed than Downton Abbey.

'Oh my goodness, that looks like Lola from the photograph,' says Charlie.

'Oh wow, yes, it does. Isn't that strange? So Anna and Lola must be the same person. Bloody hell, this is confusing. Lola could be a nickname.'

'But Lola is the name she does her taxidermy under; it must be her real name.'

'Come on,' says Juan, getting out of the car and heading towards the house. 'There's only one way to determine if this is Anna, Lola, or someone else entirely.'

'Sorry to interrupt, but are you Anna?' he says. 'No,' she replies sharply. 'No, I'm not.'

'Oh right - Lola?'

'Yes, who are you?' she replies.

'It's complicated,' says Juan. 'But we mean you no harm at all. We're just trying to solve a bit of a puzzle.'

'OK,' she says.

Charlie and I are standing behind Juan as he tries to explain this complicated situation. He tells her about Charlie moving in with Mike, while Charlie nods.

'She loves him a great deal,' he says.

'I do,' says Charlie.

'But she found these letters and wants to ensure he isn't two-timing her.'

Charlie steps forward and holds out the letters.

'Oh my God!' Lola gasps. 'Christ. How on earth did you get my letters to Michael? Who are you?'

'My name's Charlie. I've just moved in with Mike and found a tin with these letters. I want to know what's going on.'

'You have just moved in with him? Where?'

'Hampton Court.'

'Hampton Court? I don't understand.'

'Yes, in a house in Hampton Court. He's been living there for a couple of years, and I've just moved in with him.'

'This is insane,' says Lola. 'Absolutely insane. I don't understand what's going on.'

'Are you having an affair with my boyfriend?' asks Charlie.

'This is complicated,' she says. 'You need to leave before Anna gets back. I can't talk to you anymore.' 'Anna? So there is an Anna who lives here?' 'Yes.'

'And why are you here?'

'I work as their nanny.'

'Are you also training to be a taxidermist,' I say. Her face lights up.

'That's right; how did you know that?'

'Oh, long story,' I say, putting my hand into my handbag and pulling out the dead fox. This Is yours...I didn't mean to take it, but I rushed out halfway through a class.

'Right. OK, thanks for this, but I have to go in and make Rosie's tea. I haven't got anything else to say. You'll have to come back another day. Anna's husband will be back soon.'

'Hang on, who's Rosie?'

'She's Anna's child. I am her nanny.'

With that, we're left standing there. The door has been firmly closed in our faces, and the situation is more confusing than ever.

'Board meeting in the car?' I suggest.

CHAPTER 19

We pile back into Charlie's golf and sit quietly, each of us waiting for the other to speak. Eventually, Charlie's voice pricks the shield of uncomfortable silence.

'Something is going on there. Did you see her face when we started asking questions?'

'Definitely,' I agree.

'She was very jumpy and desperate for us to get away from there before Anna's husband returns.

'Yep - the last thing she needs is Anna's rich husband finding out that both his wife and nanny have been having an affair with the same guy,' says Juan.

'I guess we must come back later when Anna gets home from work.'

'No, I think we should stay here,' says Charlie. 'Let's hang around until her husband gets home and talk to him.'

'We're going to need drinks and snacks,' I say. 'Shall I go and find a corner store?'

'No, we can do better than that,' says Charlie, starting up

the engine and driving up the road. 'I saw a chip shop earlier. Let's go mad.'

I swear to God, there can be no finer words in the English language...I feel a sense of pure joy rise through my stomach until it reaches my brain, and I feel heady and slightly faint with the excitement of it all as I ponder the options. Obviously, I will have chips with curry sauce, because that's the main point of going to a chip shop, but what else...fish, a pie, saveloy, sausage? I like saveloys, but I know that Charlie will make a face and tell me they are all plastic. I think I'll go with a pie. I hope their portions of chips are big because I like chips a lot.

'Here we are,' says Charlie, and I'm out of the door before she's turned off the engine. I'm in the shop, and the smell of vinegar hits me. Oh my God. This is my drug. My knees are weak, and my palms are sweaty, and I've placed an order for chicken pie and an extra large portion of chips with curry sauce before the other two have come into the shop.

'What are you having?' I ask Charlie.

'Just a small piece of fish, and I only want a handful of chips, so don't get me a whole portion; I'll have a few of yours.'

Er..that's not going to be happening.

'Cod and chips,' I say to the chip man.

'If you can't finish them, I will,' I say to Charlie, and I feel a rush of excitement inside that I might have bagged myself a few more chips.

Juan also orders a small fish and chips, and we stand back and watch as batter and potato sizzle and dance in the boiling fat in front of us.

I grab the bag once all the food's inside it, thrusting my card towards the man behind the counter. He could charge me £200, and I wouldn't care right now; I want to be in the back of the car with the loveliest food on earth.

Once I'm settled down, and before even stopping to put my seatbelt on, I have my hand in the carrier bag to peel back the paper on the top portion and pull out a handful of chips.

'Let's not open them in here,' says Charlie. 'I don't want the car to stink of chips.'

'There is no finer smell in the world,' I counter but Char- lie's not having any of it. She wants us to sit on the bench at the end of Anna's road and eat them there.

Suddenly the drive seems like such a long way as I stare down at the drugs, I mean the chips - in front of me.

'Just here,' says Charlie, and I'm out of the car and onto the bench, taking out the joyful packages in no time. I can tell immediately which one is mine - it's twice the size of the others.

'There you go, you two,' I say, pushing their smaller packages towards them.

'Did we get cutlery?' asks Charlie.

The thought never occurred to me for a second.

'Damn, we forgot to get drinks.' says Juan. 'Shall I wander back there and get some.'

'It doesn't matter about any of that. We have chips,' I want to shout. 'That's all we need.'

Eventually, the two of them sit down and slowly open their parcels. By this stage, I've got mine ripped apart and have poured the curry sauce everywhere and am enjoying the delicious taste of warm, vinegary chips with their legs and bottoms dipped in curry sauce.

'Golly, you were hungry, Mary,' says Juan. 'I didn't realise...you should have said something.'

The truth is, I'm not really hungry. At least, I don't think

I am. I've completely lost track with what hunger is. I love eating so much and relish every piece of food so much that I don't know whether that's hunger or just an insane desire to eat.

I've just stuffed eight chips into my mouth and am delighting in the flavours and textures and feeling high from the sheer joy of it all when a car pulls up, and a man steps out. I recognise that man.

'Charlie,' I mumble as I try chewing the fried potato. 'Look.'

Charlie and Juan look over to see Mike step out of his car.

'He's with someone,' I say, seeing a figure in the passenger seat.

The figure climbs out slowly and turns around as he closes the door.

'Oh, My Fucking God. That's Ted.'

CHAPTER 20

The sight of Ted casually climbing out of Mike's car and being part of this atrocious mess is so alarming that I put down my chips and stand up from the bench. There aren't many things that can drag me from my chips.

I shout Ted's name, and he spins around...the confusion on his face, even from this distance, is plain for all to see. 'What are you doing here?' he says.

'What are YOU doing here?' I reply.

'Meeting Mike.'

Charlie walks towards me, and Mike sees her. It's like he's frozen to the spot.

'Charlie? What are you doing here?' he says. 'What on earth is going on? Why are you at my house?'

'Your house? So this is your house?' she says.

'Well, yes - but it's complicated. Just go home, all of you, and I'll explain everything when we're back in Hampton Court.'

'I'm not going anywhere, Mike. I'm not moving until you explain what's going on.'

'I'm a bit confused as well, mate,' says Ted. 'How is this your house? And - Mary, why aren't you in Wales?'

'She's not in Wales because I found these,' says Charlie, brandishing the pile of letters...the source of all the trouble.

'They are my private letters. What on earth are you doing with them?'

'I found them,' said Charlie.

'You mean - you went snooping through all my things.'

'No. We share a house, so I'm allowed to go and look in the wardrobe to put my things away. And there they were.'

'No - they were tucked away in MY wardrobe. I told you to use the other wardrobe.'

'So you admit you were trying to hide the letters from me, then.'

'No, not really, this is quite ridiculous.'

'I still don't understand what you're doing here, Mary,' says Ted. 'Last time I saw you, you were in Wales.'

'We came to Oxford to determine what was going on. How about you? Why are you here?'

'I don't want to say.'

'Oh great. That's just wonderful.'

No one seems to be getting anywhere as we stand in the street, two groups growling at one another.

To the side of us, a convertible car pulls up, and a gorgeous auburn-haired woman steps out, shaking her head so that the curls fall loosely over her shoulders. She looks like she's in an advert as she flicks her sunglasses onto the end of her nose and walks towards us.

'Noooo,' shouts Mike, running in our direction. 'Anna - go straight into the house; these people are mad.'

'Oh, thanks,' I mumble.

'I know her,' says Anna, removing her glasses and pointing at me. 'The one with sauce all over her face - she's completely mad. She turned up at the hospital with a fake injury and came on our pub crawl with a dead fox, pretending to be Nigerian. She's a lunatic.'

'Mary, what have you been up to?' asks Ted. 'And you do have a lot of sauce on your face; what is that?'

'Nothing. Just curry sauce. And don't make me out to be the bad guy here; I was trying to get close to Anna to find out what was going on with her and Mike.'

'What do you mean, Mary?' says Ted. 'Nothing's going on between Mike and anyone but Charlie. Why are you so convinced that Mike's up to no good? This is ridiculous.'

'Who is Charlie?' asks Anna. 'And what's she got to do with anything? And those letters don't look like they're from me at all. That's not my handwriting.'

'No, that one's from Lola,' says Charlie.

'Lola? My nanny?'

'Yes, I didn't realise she was your nanny. I went to talk to her yesterday and ended up doing her taxidermy class. That's why I had a dead fox under my arm when you saw me.'

'A dead fox?' says Ted. 'Honestly, Mary, what is going on?'

'There are letters from you here as well, Anna,' says Charlie. 'Letters to my boyfriend, so I suggest you tell me what's happening.'

'I have never written to anyone's boyfriend,' shouts Anna, she sounds angry, but I don't have an overwhelming amount of sympathy, she's pregnant with another man's child, and she shouldn't be sending love letters to anyone but him. 'Who is your boyfriend anyway?'

'Him,' says Charlie, pointing to Mike.

'That's Michael, my husband, we've been married for ten

years, and we have a little girl and another one on the way. How dare you...'

The commotion brings Lola into the doorway, and Anna soon turns her attention to her.

'Have you been sending love letters to Michael?' she bellows.

Lola looks even paler than usual as she stands there without speaking.

I look over at Mike.

'Are you going to explain yourself,' I say.

'I can't,' he says, his shoulders slumping forward. He looks beaten.

'Are you married to Anna?' I ask.

'Yes.'

'And are you having an affair with Lola?'

'Yes.'

Anna screams and races towards the door where Lola is standing, looking like a frightened deer. 'How could you?' she bellows. 'How could you?'

'He lives with me in Hampton Court,' says Charlie, directing her comments towards Anna but looking at Mike.

'I'm so sorry,' he says. 'I'm sorry.'

Ted has rushed to the doorway to break up the warring women while the rest of us are silent. Then Charlie starts sobbing...gently at first, but then more heavily until she's crying her eyes out.

'Come on,' I say. 'Let's go.'

Mike walks towards his front door and says something to Ted before Ted walks away and follows Charlie and me to the car.

'This is crazy; why didn't you tell me you were coming here?' he says.

'Oh, and why didn't you tell me that you and the three-timing tosspot were suddenly the greatest of friends?'

'I was planning a surprise for you,' he says.

'Yeah, of course, you were.'

'I was, honestly. I promise.'

We get to the car, and Charlie climbs into the driving seat. 'I've gone right off these,' she says, holding up her packet of fish and chips.

'Give them to me; I'll get rid of them,' I say.

'Yeah, I don't want these either.' Juan hands me his, and I lay them to the side of me.

Ted slides onto the back seat.

'You still haven't told me what you were doing there. With that scumbag.'

'I'll tell you later.'

'Tell her now,' says Charlie, with considerable aggression. 'There's no need to hold anything back for me. Nothing could make this worse. He's got a wife and kids and is already having an affair. What the fuck was I?'

'He couldn't resist you,' says Juan.

'But he has a wife, children, and a lover.'

'I know,' says Juan. 'I know.'

'I think Juan's right,' I chime in. 'He must have fallen head over heels to have taken a risk like that.'

'Look - I know you're trying to make me feel better, but he's a shit, and that's the end of it. Unless you want to add anything to the debate, Ted?'

'I didn't know about any of this. I called Mike and asked him whether he could do me a favour, that's all.'

'And you don't want to tell us what that favour was?'

'Later,' he says, laying his hand on my knee.

We arrive back at the B&B and walk into the reception.

Charlie runs in, darting towards the lift to go up to her room.

'I need to be alone,' she says as she goes. 'JUST LEAVE ME ALONE.'

Juan, Ted and I slump down into the chairs in reception.

I'm still clutching the packets of chips, and I'm dying to run upstairs to my room, lie on the bed and devour them all. I don't even want to look at Ted. How the hell is he all caught up in this mess?

'What do you think we should do about Charlie?' asks Juan. 'Shall we go up and see if she's alright.'

'Maybe just leave her for a bit,' says Ted.

His suggestion is sensible, but I'm not in the mood to be nice.

'No one asked you,' I bark at him.

'I'm just trying to help.'

'Sure you are.'

Ted holds his hands out in front of him. 'I'm not the bad guy here,' he says. 'I've not been unfaithful to you, and I never will be.'

'But you were with Mike, and you lied about where you were.'

'Because I wanted to surprise you,' he says. 'I had a plan.'

'Sure. And you knew all about Mike's lovely home life in Oxford, and it didn't occur to you to mention it to me.'

'No, I knew nothing about that. Come with me.'

Juan looks on anxiously as Ted leads me outside. We find a bench overlooking the scruffy car park, and he takes my hand: 'Look, Mary, when I heard that Mike was a fantastic jeweller, I asked him whether he could help me choose a ring for you.'

'A ring? What?'

He puts his hand into his pocket.

'He told me that if I came to his workshop, he'd show me all the rings he has. That's why I'm here. I knew nothing about him having a family here, an affair, or anything. I just wanted to get something nice for you.

'Here, this is the ring I chose. It's an eternity ring to show how much I love you and to show my commitment to being with you forever.'

The ring is stunning. It's a simple band with a large emerald held in place by a pretty setting that looks like petals are folded around the base of the gem.

'I've never seen anything so beautiful,' I say.

'Can I have some of those chips?' he replies.

I hand him the two spare packets of chips as a sign of my utter devotion to him. He tucks in while I sit back and admire the gem sparkling away on my hand.

Then, obviously, I take it off and get stuck into the chips.

CHAPTER 21

'Charlie, Charlie, is everything OK?'

The three of us are standing outside Charlie's bedroom door, knocking gently.

'I'm fine,' she says. 'I'm coming now.'

She opens the door and invites us all in. The letters are lying across the bed alongside the ripped-up photograph of Lola.

'It's over,' she says. 'Obviously, it's over. There's no way I'm having anything to do with him after that. He can stay here with his ever-so-beautiful wife in his gorgeous house and shag every nanny they employ for the rest of time. I DON'T CARE.'

'He's a complete shit,' I say. 'A real louse.'

'I know. I thought he was 'the one', you know. I thought this was it. He's so kind to me, so gentlemanly and generous.'

'He was never generous with his time, though,' I say wisely. 'He has loads of money, so he was happy to buy you lots of things, but he was hardly ever around. We only met him once, for God's sake.'

'Yeah, that's true,' she says. 'He was always busy going somewhere, unable to make it home or meet my friends...Now I know exactly where he was going.'

'Forget about him,' says Ted. 'You are lovely; you'll find someone fabulous in no time. That shit doesn't deserve a moment more of your time.'

'What were you doing here, Ted? Why were you at his house? I don't understand that at all.'

Ted holds my hand out so they can see the ring.

'I asked him whether he could design an eternity ring for me. He told me to come to his workshop and see whether there was one I liked. That's why I was here. He said he had a lovely box for it at a house round the corner, so we were going to pick the box up when we bumped into you.'

'Oh,' says Charlie. 'That's very beautiful.'

'I know,' I say. 'I feel bad about wearing it now, though.'

'Don't be daft; I'm pleased for you. I'm glad that one of us has got herself a decent man.' She looks up and smiles at me. 'You've got yourself a good one there, haven't you?'

'Yep,' I say, looking at the ring, then at Ted.

'And you will find an amazing man too. I know it probably feels like the last thing you want to do, but one day you'll meet someone lovely, just like I have.'

'Yeah, meeting someone isn't quite at the top of my to-do list. Right now, I have to get all my stuff out of his house and move it somewhere. Christ knows where I'm going to live.'

'I'll help you to get your belongings out of the house,' says Ted. 'And you can stay with us while you find somewhere to live.'

'Thank you,' says Charlie. 'That's such relief. My old place has been rented out. This is a bloody disaster.'

'No!' says Juan, interrupting in a great fluster of arms

and jazz hands. 'No, it's not a disaster. Not a disaster at all. It's perfect.'

'Is it? How is it perfect?'

'You can come and live with me. I need a flatmate, and as long as you don't wear nappies and can put up with large antlers on the wall, the room's all yours.'

'Oh, that would be great,' says Charlie, jumping up to hug Juan. 'And we'll have far more fun than I'd ever have had with that tosser.'

'We will have such fun. I want to decorate the whole place...what do you think?'

'Oh yes, that would be brill.'

'Pink kitchen?' says Juan. 'I love a pink kitchen.' 'Yes. And chandeliers. My God, I love chandeliers so much.'

'Me too!' squeals Juan. 'I have found my style partner.'

The two of them hug, and I admit to feeling left out of all the fun. I mean - Ted's great, and I love him with all my heart, but he's never going to get excited about a pink kitchen with chandeliers, is he?

'We could have a moving-in party,' says Charlie, and suddenly they're jumping up and down and discussing invitations covered in glitter.

'Who needs Mike?' says Juan.

'Oh, let's get a neon sign saying that and put it in the hallway. I can picture it now...a giant green 'Who needs Mike?' sign. '

'And send him a picture of it in pride of place. Oh - we are going to have SO MUCH fun,' Juan says, almost heady with excitement.

'I know. We're going to be best friends.'

'We will too, angel,' says Ted, wrapping his arm around me. 'We're going to have lots of fun. I promise you.'

Want to read more about Mary Brown?

Of course, you do!

The next book is called: **DOG DAYS FOR MARY BROWN.**

Available now: My Book

This is what it's all about...

'Hey, Mary. Get a puppy.' They all said. 'He will love you as no one has ever loved you before.'

Three weeks later, the furniture is chewed to pieces, half my shoes and socks are missing, the house training is not going well, and when I took him to a restaurant, he started humping the waiter's leg. I had to pull him off as he clung on with his claws, still humping the air as I pulled him off.

My puppy has worked out how to climb out of his car seat, and he barks like mad if he sees anyone in a hat.

It's like a madhouse here. No one tells you about this stuff.

They also don't tell you that a whole new community opens up to you when you have a puppy. And not all the people in that community are friendly...

They also don't tell you that if your puppy goes missing, it will be the WORST THING EVER.

You'll feel like your heart is breaking as you think about those gorgeous, chocolate-brown eyes that melt your heart, and you won't be able to stop thinking about the way he does a little skip when he's running through the park and the way he lies on his back when he wants tickles.

And you'll realise you will do anything, ANYTHING, to get him back.

Published internationally by Gold Medals Media Ltd. © Bernice Bloom 2022

Terms and Conditions:

The purchaser of this book is subject to the condition that he/she shall in no way resell it, nor any part of it, nor make copies of it to distribute freely.

All Persons Fictitious Disclaimer:

This book is a work of fiction. Any similarity between the characters and situations within its pages and places or persons, living or dead, is unintentional and coincidental.

Printed in Great Britain
by Amazon